MEG CABOT

THE PRINCESS DIARIES

PROM PRINCESS

MACMILLAN

First published in the UK 2003 by Macmillan Children's Books

This edition published 2015 by Macmillan Children's Books
an imprint of Pan Macmillan
20 New Wharf Road, London N1 9RR
Associated companies throughout the world
www.panmacmillan.com

ISBN 978-1-4472-8776-6

1 3 5 7 9 8 6 4 2

A CIP catalogue record for this book is available from the British Library.

Typeset by Nigel Hazle
Printed and bound by CPI Group (UK) Ltd, Croydon CR0 4YY

Many thanks to the usual suspects: Beth Ader, Jennifer Brown, Barb Cabot, Sarah Davies, Laura Langlie, Abby McAden, David Walton and especially Benjamin Egnatz.

'It's true,' she said. 'Sometimes I do pretend I am a princess. I pretend I am a princess, so that I can try and behave like one.'

A *Little Princess*, Frances Hodgson Burnett

The Atom

The Official Student-Run Newspaper of Albert Einstein High School

Take *Pride* in the AEHS Lions

Week of May 5   *Volume 456/Issue 27*

Science Fair Winners Announced

by Rafael Menendez

Science students entered 21 projects in the Albert Einstein High School Science Fair. Several projects advanced to the New York City regional competition, which will be held next month. Senior Judith Gershner received the grand prize for slicing a human genome. Earning special honours were senior Michael Moscovitz for his computer program modelling the death of a dwarf star, and freshman Kenneth Showalter for his experiments in gender transfiguration in newts.

Lacrosse Teams Win

by Ai-Lin Hong

Both the varsity and junior varsity lacrosse teams beat their competitors this past weekend. Senior Josh Richter led the varsity team to a stunning defeat of The Dwight School 7–6 in overtime. The JV defeated Dwight by a score of 8–0. These exciting games were marred by a peculiarly aggressive Central Park squirrel that continuously darted out on to the field. Eventually it was chased away by Principal Gupta.

AEHS's Princess Spends Spring Break Building Homes for Appalachian Poor

by Melanie Greenbaum

Spring Break was a working holiday for AEHS freshman Mia Thermopolis. Mia, who, it was revealed last fall, is actually the sole heir to the throne of the principality of Genovia, spent her five-day vacation helping to build homes for Housing for the Homeless. Said the princess of her sojourn in the foothills of the Smoky Mountains, 'It was OK. Except for the whole "no bathroom" thing. And the part where I kept hitting myself on the thumb with my hammer.'

Senior Week

by Josh Richter, Senior Class President

The week of May 5–10 is Senior Week. This is the time to honour this year's AEHS graduating class, who have worked so hard to show you leadership throughout the year. The Senior Week Events Calendar goes like this:

Mon	Tues	Wed	Thurs	Fri	Sat
Senior Awards Banquet	Senior Sports Banquet	Senior Debate	Senior Skit Nite	Senior Skip Day	Senior Prom

A Note From Your Principal:

Senior Skip Day is not an event sanctioned by school administration. All students are required to attend classes Friday 9 May. In addition, the request made by certain members of the freshman class to lift the sanction against underclassmen attending the prom unless invited by an upperclassman is denied.

Notice to all Students:

It has come to the attention of the administration that many pupils do not seem to know the proper words to the AEHS School Song. They are as follows:

> *Einstein Lions, we're for you!*
> *Come on, be bold, come on,*
> *be bold, come on, be bold!*

> *Einstein Lions, we're for you!*
> *Blue and gold, blue and gold,*
> *blue and gold!*

> *Einstein Lions, we're for you!*
> *We've got a team no one else*
> *can ever tame!*

> *Einstein Lions, we're for you*
> *Let's win this game!*

Please note that at this year's graduation ceremony, any student caught singing alternative (particularly explicit and/or suggestive) words to the AEHS School Song will be removed from the premises. Complaints that the AEHS School Song is too militaristic must be submitted in writing to the AEHS administrative office, not scrawled on toilet doors or discussed on any student's public access television programme.

Letters to the Editor:

To Whom it May Concern: Melanie Greenbaum's article in last week's issue of *The Atom* on the strides the women's movement has made in the past three decades was laughably facile. Sexism is still alive and well, not only around the world, but in our own country. In Utah, for instance, polygamous marriages involving brides as young as eleven years of age are thriving, practised by fundamentalist Mormons who continue to live by traditions their ancestors brought west in the mid-1800s. The number of people in polygamous families in Utah is estimated by human rights groups at perhaps as many as 50,000, despite the fact that polygamy is not tolerated by the mainstream Mormon church, and also that the enforcement of tough penalties in the case of underage brides can sentence a polygamous husband or church leader arranging such a marriage to up to fifteen years in prison. I am not telling other cultures how to live, or anything. I am just saying take off the rose-coloured spectacles, Ms Greenbaum, and write an article about some of the real problems that affect half the population of this planet. The staff of *The Atom* might well consider giving some of their other writers a chance to report on these issues, instead of relegating them to the cafeteria beat.

Lilly Moscovitz

AEHS Food Court Menu
compiled by Mia Thermopolis

Monday	Tuesday	Wednesday	Thursday	Friday
Potato Bar	Soup & Sand.	Taco Salad Bar	Asian Bar	Bean Bar
Fr. Bread Pizza	Chicken Pattie	Burrito	Chicken Parm	Grilled Cheese
Fish Fingers	Tuna in Pitta	Corndog/Pickle	Corn/FF	Curly Fries
Meatball Sub	Indiv. Pizza	Deli Bar	Pasta Bar	Buffalo Bites
Spicy Chix	Nachos Deluxe	Italian Beef	Fish Stix	Soft Pretzel

Happy Ad
Go to the prom with me, CF?
Please say yes.
GD

Lost: Spiral notebook in caf., on or about 4/27. Read and DIE! Reward for safe return.
Locker No. 510

Happy Ad
Happy birthday in advance, MT!
Love,
Your Loyal Subjects

Happy Ad
Shop at Ho's Deli for all your school supply needs! New this week: ERASERS, STAPLES, NOTEBOOKS, PENS. Also Yu-Gi-Oh cards, *Slimfast* in Strawberry

---

For Sale:
One Fender precision bass, baby-blue, never been played. On or about 4/27. Read and with amp, how-to guides. $300.
Locker No. 345

Looking for Love:
Female frosh, loves romance/reading, wants older boy who enjoys same. Must be taller than 5'8", no mean people, non-smokers only. NO METALHEADS.
Email: Iluvromance@aehs.edu

Happy Ad
Personal to MK from MW:
My love for you
Like a flower grows
Where it will stop
No one knows.

4

Wednesday. April 30. Bio.

Mia – Did you see the latest issue of *The Atom*?

> I know, Shameeka, I just got my copy. I wish Lilly would stop mentioning me in her letters to the editor. I mean, as the only freshman on the newspaper staff, I have to pay my dues. Lesley Cho, the editor-in-chief, got her start on the cafeteria beat. I am TOTALLY FINE with covering the lunch menu every week.

Well, I think Lilly just feels if your goal really is to be a writer someday, you aren't going to get there writing about Buffalo Bites!

> That is not true. I have made some very important innovations in the lunch column. For instance, it was my idea to capitalize the 'i' in Individual Pizza.

Lilly is only looking out for your best interests.

> Whatever. Melanie Greenbaum is on the girls' basketball team. She could fully slam-dunk me if she wanted to. I don't think Lilly antagonizing her is in my best interests.

So . . .

So what?

So has he asked you yet?????

Has who asked me what?

HAS MICHAEL ASKED YOU TO THE
PROM???????

Oh. No.

Mia, the prom is in less than TWO WEEKS!
Jeff asked me a MONTH ago. How are
you going to get your dress in time if you
don't find out soon whether or not you're
going? Plus you have to make an appointment
to get your hair and nails done, and get the
boutonnière, and he has to rent the limo and
his tux and make dinner reservations. This is
not pizza at Bowlmore Lanes, you know. It's
dinner and dancing at Maxim's! It's serious!

I'm sure Michael is going to ask me soon. He has
a lot on his mind, what with the new band and
college in the autumn and all.

Well, you better light a fire under him.

Because you don't want to end up having him ask at the last minute. Because then if you say yes it'll be like you were waiting around for him to ask.

Hello, Michael and I are going out. It's not like I'm going to go with somebody else. As if anybody else would ask me. I mean, I'm not YOU, Shameeka. I don't have all these senior guys lined up at my locker, just waiting for a chance to ask me out. Not that I would. Go out with another guy, I mean. If one asked. Because I love Michael with every fibre of my being.

Well, I hope he asks you soon, because I don't want to be the only freshman girl at the prom! Who will I hang with in the ladies' room?

Don't worry. I'll be there. Oops. What was that about ice worms?

They differ from earthworms in that they . . .

The Ice Worm
by
Mia Thermopolis*

Contrary to popular opinion, glaciers do not just support life above and below them, but also within them.

Recently, scientists discovered the existence of worms that live *inside* ice – even mounds of methane ice on the floor of the Gulf of Mexico. These creatures, called ice worms, are one to two inches long and live off the chemosynthetic bacteria that grow on the methane, or are otherwise living symbiotically with them . . .

Only 70 words. 180 to go.

HOW CAN I THINK ABOUT ICE WORMS WHEN MY BOYFRIEND HASN'T ASKED ME TO THE PROM???????

*Mr Sturgess, the notes Shameeka and I were passing were fully class-related. I swear. But whatever.

Wednesday, April 30, Health and Safety

M – Why do you look like you just swallowed a sock?

> Because, Lilly, the Bio sub caught
> Shameeka and me passing notes and
> assigned us both a 250-word paper on
> ice worms.

So? You should look at it as an artistic challenge. Besides,
250 words is nothing for an ace journalist like yourself. You
should be able to knock that out in half an hour.

> Lilly, has your brother mentioned the prom
> to you?

Um. What?

> Prom. You know. Senior Prom. The one
> they are holding at Maxim's a week from
> this Saturday. Has he mentioned to you
> whether or not he's, um, planning on asking
> anyone?

ANYONE? Just who do you mean by ANYONE? His DOG?

> You know what I mean.

Michael does not discuss things like the prom with me, Mia. Mainly what Michael discusses with me is whether or not it is my turn to empty the dishwasher, set the table, or take the wadded-up tissues down the hall to the incinerator chute after Mom and Dad's Adult Survivors of Childhood Alien Abduction group therapy meetings.

Oh. Well, I was just wondering.

Don't worry, Mia. If Michael's going to ask anyone to the prom, it will be you.

What do you mean IF Michael's going to ask anyone to the prom?

I meant WHEN. OK? What is WITH you?

Nothing. Only that Michael is my one true love and he's graduating and so if we don't go to the prom this year I'll never get to go. Unless we go when I'M a senior, but that won't be for THREE YEARS!!!!!!!!!!
And, besides, by that time Michael might be in graduate school. He might have a beard or something!!!!! You can't go to the prom with someone who has a BEARD.

10

I can see that you're very emotional about this. Are you premenstrual or something?

> NO!!!!!! I JUST WANT TO GO TO THE PROM WITH MY BOYFRIEND BEFORE HE GRADUATES AND/OR GROWS EXCESSIVE AMOUNTS OF FACIAL HAIR!!!!!!!! IS THERE ANYTHING WRONG WITH THAT??????

Whoa. You fully need to take a Midol. And rather than asking me whether or not I think my brother is going to ask you to the prom, I think you should ask YOURSELF something, and that's why a completely outdated, pagan dance ritual is so important to you.

> It's just important to me, OK????

Is this because of that time your mom wouldn't buy you the Prom Queen Glamour Gown for your Barbie, and you had to make your own out of toilet paper?

> HELLO!!!! Lilly, I would think that you might have noticed that the prom plays a key role in the socialization process of the adolescent. I mean, look at all the movies that have been made about it:

Movies That Feature the Prom as Prominent Plot Device

by Mia Thermopolis

Pretty in Pink: Will Molly Ringwald go to the prom with the cute rich boy or the poor weird boy? Whichever one she goes with, does she really think he's going to like that hideous pink potato sack of a dress she makes?

Ten Things I Hate About You: Julia Stiles and Heath Ledger. Was there ever a more perfect couple? I think not. It just takes the prom to prove it to them.

Valley Girl: Nicholas Cage's first starring role in a movie ever, and he plays a punk rocker who crashes a suburban mall rat's prom. Who will she ride home with in the limo, the guy with the Members Only jacket, or the guy with the Mohawk? What happens at the prom will decide it.

Footloose: Who can forget Kevin Bacon in the immortal role of Ren, convincing the kids in the town with the no-dancing ordinance to rent a place outside city limits so they can assert their independence by tripping the light *fantastique* to Kenny Loggins?

She's All That: Rachael Leigh Cook has to go to the prom in order to prove that she is not as big a nerd as everyone thinks she is. And then it turns out she still is, but — and this is the best part of the whole thing — Freddie Prinze Junior loves her anyway!!!!!

Never Been Kissed: Girl reporter Drew Barrymore goes undercover to crash a masquerade prom! Her friends dress as a strand of DNA, but Drew knows better and wins the heart of the teacher she loves by dressing as, what else, a princess (oh, OK, Rosalind. But it looks like a princess costume).

And who can forget:

Back to the Future: If Michael J. Fox doesn't get his parents together by the prom, he might not ever be BORN!!!!!!!!! Proving the importance of the prom from both a societal as well as a BIOLOGICAL point of view!

What about *Carrie*? Or do you not count buckets of pig blood as essential to the adolescent socialization process?

YOU KNOW WHAT I MEAN!!!!!!!!!

OK, OK, calm down, I get your point.

> You're just jealous because Boris can't ask you
> because he's still just a freshman like us!

I am making sure you get some protein at lunch because I think
your vegetarianism has finally short-circuited your brain cells.
You need meat, now.

> Why are you minimalizing my pain? I have a
> legitimate concern here, and I think you need to
> consider the fact that it has nothing to do with
> my diet or menstrual cycle.

I seriously think you need to lie down with your feet above your
head to get the blood flowing back into your brain because you
are suffering from severe cognitive impairment.

> Lilly, SHUT UP! I am way stressed right now!
> I mean, tomorrow is my fifteenth birthday,
> and I am still nowhere close to becoming self-
> actualized. Nothing is going right in my life: my
> father is insisting that I spend July and August
> with him in Genovia; my home life is completely
> unsatisfactory, what with my pregnant mother's
> incessant references to her bladder, and her

insistence on giving birth to my future brother or sister at home, in the LOFT, with only a midwife — a midwife! — in attendance; my boyfriend is graduating from high school and starting college, where he will constantly be thrust into the presence of large-busted co-eds in black turtlenecks who like to talk about Kant, and my best friend doesn't seem to understand why the prom is important to me!!!!!!!!!!!!

You forgot to complain about your grandmother.

No, I didn't. Grandmère has been in Palm Springs having a chemical face peel. She won't be back until tonight.

Mia, I thought you prided yourself on the fact that you and Michael had this open and honest relationship. Why don't you just ask him yourself if he plans on going?

I CAN'T DO THAT! I mean, then it will sound like I am asking him to ask me.

No, it won't.

Yes, it will.

No, it won't.

Yes, it will.

No, it won't. And not all co-eds have large breasts. You really ought to speak to a mental health specialist about this absurd fixation you have with the size of your chest. It's not healthy.

Oh, there's the bell, THANK GOD!!!!!!

Wednesday, April 30, Gifted and Talented

IT IS NOT FAIR. I mean, I know my friends have more important things on their minds than the prom — Michael is busy with graduation and Skinner Box, his band; Lilly's got her TV show which, even if it is still only on the public access channel, continues to break new ground in television news journalism every week; Tina's still looking for a guy to replace her ex, Dave Farouq El-Abar, in her heart; Shameeka's got cheerleading, and Ling Su has Art Club and all.

But, HELLO!!!!!!! Isn't ANYONE thinking about the prom? ANYONE AT ALL, besides me and Shameeka??? I mean, it is next week, and Michael hasn't asked me yet. NEXT WEEK!!!! Shameeka is right: if we are going, we really have to start planning for it now.

Only how am I supposed to ask Michael whether or not he is planning on asking me? You can't do that. That fully ruins the romance of the thing. I mean, it's bad enough that my own mother was the one who had to propose when she found out she was pregnant. When I asked her how Mr G popped the question, my mom said he didn't. She said the conversation went like this:

Helen Thermopolis: 'Frank, I'm pregnant.'

Mr Gianini: 'Oh. OK. What do you want to do?'

Helen Thermopolis: 'Marry you.'

Mr Gianini: 'OK.'

HELLO!!!!!!!!! Where is the romance in THAT???? 'Frank, I'm pregnant, let's get married.' 'OK.' AAAAACKKKK!!!!
 What about:

Helen Thermopolis: 'Frank, the seed from your loins has sprung to fruition in my womb.'

Mr Gianini: 'Helen, I have never heard such joyous news in all of my thirty-nine years. Will you do me the very great honour of becoming my bride, my soul mate, my life partner?'

Helen Thermopolis: 'Yes, my sweet protector.'

Mr Gianini: 'My life! My hope! My love!' (KISS)

That's how it SHOULD have gone. Look at the difference. It is so much better when the guy asks the girl instead of the girl asking the guy.
 So, obviously, I can't just walk up to Michael and be all:

Mia Thermopolis: 'So are we going to the prom or what? 'Cause I need to buy my dress.'

Michael Moscovitz: 'OK.'

NO!!!!!!!!! That will never work!!!!!!! Michael has to ask ME. He has to be all:

Michael Moscovitz: 'Mia, the past five months have been the most magical of my life. Being with you is like having a refreshing ocean breeze blowing constantly against my passion-fevered brow. You are my sole reason for living, the purpose for which my heart beats. It would be the greatest honour of my life if I could escort you to the Senior Prom, where you must promise to dance every single dance with me, except the fast ones that we will sit down during because they are lame.'

Mia Thermopolis: 'Oh, Michael, this is so sudden! I simply wasn't expecting it. But I adore you with every fibre of my being, so of course I will go to the prom with you, and dance every single dance with you, except the fast ones because they are lame.' (KISS)

That's how it should go. If there is any justice in the world, that's how it WILL go.

But WHEN? When is he going to ask me? I mean, look at him over there. He is so clearly NOT thinking about the prom. He is arguing with Boris Pelkowski over the rhythm of their band's new song, 'Rock-throwing Youths', a searing criticism of the current situation in the Middle East. I am sorry, but someone who is worrying about the situation in the Middle East is HARDLY LIKELY TO REMEMBER TO ASK HIS GIRLFRIEND TO THE PROM.

This is what I get for falling in love with a genius.

Not that Michael isn't a perfectly attentive boyfriend. I mean, I know a lot of girls — like Tina, for instance — are totally jealous of me for having such a hot and yet so incredibly supportive life mate. I mean, Michael ALWAYS sits next to me at lunch, every single day, except Tuesdays and Thursdays when he has a Computer Club meeting during lunch. But even then he gazes at me longingly from the Computer Club table on the other side of the caf.

Well, OK, maybe not longingly, but he smiles at me sometimes when he catches me staring at him from across the cafeteria, trying to figure out who he looks like the most, Josh Hartnett or a dark-haired Heath Ledger.

And, OK, so Michael doesn't feel comfortable with public displays of affection — which is no big surprise seeing as how everywhere I go I am followed by a six-foot-five Swedish expert in krav maga — so it's not like he ever kisses me in school or holds hands in the hallway or sticks his hand in the back pocket of my overalls when we are strolling down the street or leans his body up against mine when we're at my locker the way Josh does to Lana . . .

But when we are alone . . . when we are alone . . . when we are alone . . .

Oh, all right, so we haven't got to second base yet. Well, except for that one time during Spring Break when we were building that house. But I think that might have been a mistake on account of my hammer was hanging by its claw from the bib of my overalls and Michael asked to borrow it and I couldn't hand it to him because I was busy holding up that sheet of dry wall so his hand sort of accidentally brushed up against my chest while he was reaching . . .

Still. We are perfectly happy together. More than happy. We are *ecstatically* happy.

SO WHY HASN'T HE ASKED ME TO THE PROM?????????????????

Oh my God. Lilly just leaned over to see what I was writing and saw that last part. That is what I get for using capital letters. She just went, 'Oh, God, don't tell me you're *still* obsessing over that.'

As if that weren't bad enough, Michael looked up and went, 'Obsessing over what?'!!!!!!!!!!!

I thought Lilly was going to say something!!!!!!!!!! I thought she was going to go, 'Oh, Mia's just having an embolism because you haven't asked her to the prom yet.'

But she just went, 'Mia's working on an essay about methane ice worms.'

Michael said, 'Oh,' and turned back to his guitar.

Trust Boris to go, 'Oh, methane ice-worms. Yes, of course. If they turn out to be ubiquitous on shallow sea-floor gas deposits, they could have a significant impact on how methane deposits are formed and dissolve in seawater, and how we go about mining and otherwise harvesting natural gas as a source of energy.'

Which, you know, is good to know for my essay and all, but seriously. Why does he even know this?

I don't know how Lilly puts up with him. I really don't.

Wednesday, April 30, French

Thank God for Tina Hakim Baba. At least SHE understands how I feel. AND she totally sympathizes. She says that it has always been her dream to go to the prom with the man she loves — like Molly Ringwald dreamed of going to the prom with Andrew McCarthy.

Sadly for Tina, however, the man she loves — or once loved — dumped her for a girl named Jasmine with turquoise braces. But Tina says she will learn to love again, if she can find a man willing to break down the self-defensive emotional wall she has built up around herself since Dave Farouq El-Abar's betrayal. It was looking like Peter Hu, whom Tina met over Spring Break, might succeed, but Peter's obsession with Korn soon drove her away, as it would any right-thinking woman.

Tina thinks Michael is going to ask tomorrow, on my birthday. About the prom, I mean. Oh, please let that be true! It would be the best birthday present anyone has ever given me. Except for when my mom gave me Fat Louie, of course.

Except I hope he doesn't do it, you know. In front of my family. Because Michael is coming out with us on my birthday. We are going to dinner tomorrow night with

23

Grandmère and my dad and Mom and Mr Gianini. Oh, and Lars, of course. And then on Saturday night my mom is having a big blow-out party for me and all my friends at the Loft (that is, providing she can still walk by then, on account of her you-know-what).

I haven't mentioned Mom's problem with her you-know-what to Michael, though. I believe in having a fully open and honest relationship with the man you love, but, seriously, there are some things he just doesn't need to know. Like that your pregnant mother has problems with her bladder.

I only invited Michael to both the dinner and the party. Everyone else, including Lilly, is just invited to the party. Hello, how unromantic would *that* be, to have your birthday dinner with your mom, your stepdad, your real dad, your grandma, your bodyguard, your boyfriend and his sister. At least I was able to narrow it down a little.

Michael said he would come to both, the dinner and the party, which I thought was very brave of him and further proof that he is the best boyfriend that ever lived.

If I could just nail him down on this prom thing, though.

Tina says I should just come out and ask him. Michael, I mean. Tina is a staunch believer in being very up front with boys, on account of how she played games with Dave and he fled from her into the arms of the turquoise-toothed Jasmine.

But I don't know. I mean, this is the PROM. The prom is special. I don't want to mess it up. Especially since I'm only going to be able to see Michael for like another month or so before my dad drags me off to Genovia for the summer. Which is so totally unfair. 'But you signed a contract, Mia,' is what he keeps saying to me. My dad, I mean.

Yeah, I signed a contract, like a *year* ago. OK, eight months ago. How was I supposed to know then that I would fall madly and passionately in love? Well, OK, I was madly and passionately in love back then, but, hello, it was with somebody totally different. And the real object of my affections didn't like me back. Or, if he did (he says he did!!!!!!!!!), I didn't exactly know it, did I?

And now my dad expects me to spend two whole months away from the man to whom I have pledged my heart?

Oh, no. I don't think so.

It is one thing to spend Christmas in Genovia. I mean, that was only thirty-two days. But July *and* August? I'm supposed to spend two whole *months* away from him?

Well, it is so not happening. My dad thinks he's being all reasonable about it, since originally he was going to make me spend the WHOLE summer in Genovia. But since Mom's due date is in June, he's acting like it's this big concession to let me stay in New York until the baby's born. Oh, yeah. Thanks, Dad.

Well, he is just going to have to exhale, because if he thinks I am spending the last two months of the first summer of my life with an actual boyfriend *away* from said boyfriend, then he is in for a very big surprise. I mean, what is there even to *do* in Genovia in the summer? NOTHING. The place is lousy with tourists (well, so is New York, but, whatever, New York tourists are different — they are much less repulsive than the ones who go to Genovia) and parliament isn't even in session. What am I going to *do* all day? I mean, at least here there'll be the whole baby thing, once my mom hurries up and has it, which I actually wish would be sooner than June because it is like living with Sasquatch. I swear to God, all she does is stomp around and grunt at us; she is in such a bad mood on account of all the water weight and the pressure on her you-know-what (my mom shares WAY too much information sometimes).

Whatever happened to pregnancy being the most magical time in a woman's life? Whatever happened to being full of the wonder and glory of creation?

Clearly my mom has never heard of either of those things.

The point is, this is Michael's last summer before he leaves for college. And, OK, the college he is going to is just a few subway stops uptown, but, whatever, I am not going to see him at school any more after this. For instance, he is no longer going to be swinging by my Algebra class to give me strawberry gummy worms like he did this morning, to the wrath of Lana Weinberger, who is just jealous because her boyfriend Josh NEVER surprises her with gummy worms.

No. Michael and I should be spending this summer together, having lovely picnics in Central Park (except that I hate having picnics in public parks because all the homeless people come around and look longingly at your egg-salad sandwich, or whatever, and then you have to give it to them because you feel so guilty about having so much when others have nothing and they are usually not even grateful — they usually say something like, 'I hate egg salad,' which is very ungracious if you ask me) and seeing *Tosca* on the Great Lawn (except that I hate opera because everybody dies all tragically at the end, but whatever). There's still strolling through the San Gennaro festival and Michael maybe winning me a stuffed animal at the air-rifle booth (except that he is ethically opposed to guns, as am I, except if you are a member of law enforcement or a soldier or whatever, and those stuffed animals they give away at fairs are fully made by children in Guatemalan sweatshops).

Still. It could have been totally romantic, if my dad hadn't gone and ruined it all.

Lilly says my father clearly has abandonment issues from

when his father died and left him all alone with Grandmère and that's why he is being so totally rigid on the whole spending-my-summer-in-Genovia thing.

Except that Grandpère died when my dad was in his twenties, not exactly his formative years, so I don't see how this is possible. But Lilly says the human psyche works in strange and mysterious ways and that I should just accept that and move on.

I think the person with issues might be Lilly on account of how it's been almost four months since her public access television programme *Lilly Tells It Like It Is* was optioned by the producers who made the movie based on my life and they still haven't managed to find a studio willing to film a pilot episode. But Lilly says the entertainment industry works in strange and mysterious ways (just like the human psyche) and that she has accepted it and moved on, just like I should about the whole Genovian thing.

BUT I WILL NEVER ACCEPT THE FACT THAT MY DAD WANTS ME TO SPEND SIXTY-TWO WHOLE DAYS AWAY FROM THE MAN I LOVE!!!! NEVER!!!!!!!!!!!!!

Tina says I should try to get a summer internship somewhere here in Manhattan, and then my dad won't be able to make me go to Genovia, on account of how that would be shirking my responsibilities here. Only I don't know of any place that would want a princess for an intern.

I mean, what would Lars do all day while I was alphabetizing files or making photocopies or whatever?

When I walked in before class started, Mademoiselle Klein was showing some of the sophomore girls a picture of this slinky dress she is ordering from Victoria's Secret to wear to the prom. She is a chaperone. So is Mr Wheeton, the track coach and my Health and Safety teacher. They are going out together. Tina says it is the most romantic thing she has ever heard of, besides my mom and Mr Gianini. I have not revealed to Tina the painful truth about my mom being the one to propose to Mr Gianini, because I don't want to crush all Tina's fondest dreams. I have also hidden from her the fact that I don't think Prince Harry is ever going to email her back. That's on account of how I gave her a fake email address for him. Well, I had to do something to get her to quit bugging me for it. And I'm sure whoever is at princeh@windsorcastle.com is very appreciative of her five-page testimonial on how much she loves him, especially when he is wearing his polo jodhpurs.

I sort of feel bad about lying to Tina, but it was only to make her feel better. And some day I really will get Prince Harry's real email address for her. I just have to wait until somebody important dies, and I see him at the state funeral. It probably won't be long — Elizabeth Taylor is looking pretty shaky.

Il me faut des lunettes de soleil.
Didier demand à essayer la jupe.

I don't know how someone who is as deeply in love with Mr Wheeton like Mademoiselle Klein is supposed to be can assign us so much homework. Whatever happened to spring, when the world is mud-luscious and the little lame balloon-man whistles far and wee?

Nobody who teaches at this school has a grain of romance in them. Ditto most of the people who go here too. Without Tina, I would be truly lost.

Jeudi, j'ai fait de l'aerobic.

Homework:
Algebra: pages 279–300
English: *The Iceman Cometh*
Biology: Finish ice-worm essay
Health and Safety: pages 154–160
Gifted and Talented: As if
French: *Ecrivez une histoire personnelle*
World Civ.: pages 310–330

Wednesday, April 30, in the limo on the way home from the Plaza

Grandmère fully knows there is something up with me. But she thinks it's because I'm upset over the whole going-to-Genovia-for-the-summer thing. As if I don't have much more immediate concerns.

'We shall have a lovely time in Genovia this summer, Amelia,' Grandmère kept saying. 'They are currently excavating a tomb they believe might belong to your ancestress, Princess Rosagunde. I understand that the mummification processes used in the 700s were really every bit as advanced as ones employed by the Egyptians. You might actually get to gaze upon the face of the woman who founded the royal house of Renaldo.'

Great. I get to spend my summer looking up some old mummy's nasal cavity. My dream come true. Oh no, sorry, Mia. No hanging out at Coney Island with your one true love for you. No fun volunteer work tutoring little kids with their reading. No cool summer job taking tourists on 'Best Pizza in NYC' food tours. No, you get to commune with a thousand-year-old corpse. Yippee!

I guess I must be more upset about the whole Michael thing than even I thought, because midway through

Grandmère's lecture on tipping (manicurists: $3; pedicurists: $5; cab drivers: $2 for rides under $10, $5 for airport trips; double the tax for restaurant bills except in states where the tax is less than 8 per cent; etc.) she went, 'AMELIA! WHAT IS THE MATTER WITH YOU?'

I must have jumped about ten feet into the air. I was totally thinking about Michael. About how good he would look in a tux. About how I could buy him a red-rose boutonnière, just the plain kind without the baby's breath because boys don't like baby's breath. And I could wear a black dress, one of those off-one-shoulder kinds like Kirsten Dunst always wears to movie premieres, with a butterfly hem and a slit up the side, and high heels with laces that go up your ankle.

Only Grandmère says black on girls under eighteen is morbid, that off-one-shoulder gowns and butterfly hems look like they were made that way accidentally, and that those lace-up high heels look like the kind of shoes Russell Crowe wore in *Gladiator* – not a flattering look on most women.

But whatever. I could fully put on body glitter. Grandmère doesn't even KNOW about body glitter.

'Amelia!' Grandmère was saying. She couldn't yell too loud because her face was still stinging from the chemical peel. I could tell because Rommel, her mostly hairless miniature poodle who looks like he's seen a chemical peel or two himself, kept leaping up into her lap and trying to lick her face, like it was a piece of raw meat or whatever. Not to gross anybody out, but that's sort of how it looked. Or like Grandmère had accidentally stepped in front of one of those hoses they used to get the radiation off Cher in that movie *Silkwood*.

'Are you listening to a single word I've said?' Grandmère looked peeved. Mostly because her face hurt, I'm sure. 'This could be very important to you some day, if you happen to be stranded without a calculator or your limo.'

'Sorry, Grandmère,' I said. I *was* sorry too. Tipping is totally my worst thing, on account of how it involves maths and also thinking quickly on your feet. When I order food from Number One Noodle Son back home I always have to ask the restaurant while I am still on the phone with them ordering how much it will be so I can work on calculating how much to tip the delivery guy before he gets to the door. Because otherwise he ends up standing there for like ten minutes while I figure out how much to give him for a seventeen dollar and fifty cent order. It's embarrassing.

'I don't know where your head's been lately, Amelia,' Grandmère said, all crabby. Well, you would be crabby too if you'd paid money to have the top two or three layers of your skin chemically removed. 'I hope you're not still worrying about your mother, and that ridiculous home birth she's planning. I told you before, your mother's forgotten what labour feels like. As soon as her contractions kick in, she'll be begging to be taken to the hospital for a nice epidural.'

I sighed. Although the fact that my mother is choosing a home birth over a nice safe clean hospital birth — where there are oxygen tanks and candy machines and Dr Kovach — *is* upsetting, I have been trying not to think about it too much . . . especially since I suspect Grandmère is right. My mother cries like a baby when she stubs her toe. How is she going to withstand hours and hours of labour pains? She was much younger when she gave birth to me. Her thirty-six-year-old body is in no shape for the rigours of childbirth. She doesn't even work out!

Grandmère fastened her evil eye on to me.

'I suppose the fact the weather's starting to get warm isn't helping,' she said. 'Young people tend to get flighty in the spring. And, of course, there's your birthday tomorrow.'

I fully let Grandmère think that's what was distracting me. My birthday and the fact that my friends and I are all twitterpated, like Thumper gets in springtime in *Bambi*.

'You are a very difficult person for whom to find a suitable birthday gift, Amelia,' Grandmère said, reaching for her Sidecar and her cigarettes. Grandmère has her cigarettes sent to her from Genovia, so she doesn't have to pay the astronomical tax on them that they charge here in New York, in the hopes of making people quit smoking on account of it being too expensive. Except that it isn't working, since all the people in Manhattan who smoke are just hopping on the PATH train and going over to New Jersey to buy their cigarettes.

'You are not the jewellery type,' Grandmère went on, lighting up and puffing away. 'And you don't seem to have any appreciation whatsoever for couture. And it isn't as if you have any hobbies.'

I pointed out to Grandmère that I do have a hobby. Not just a hobby, even, but a *calling*: I write.

Grandmère just waved her hand, and said, 'But not a *real* hobby. You don't play golf or paint.'

It kind of hurt my feelings that Grandmère doesn't think writing is a real hobby. She is going to be very surprised when I grow up and become a published author. Then writing will not only be my hobby, but my career. Maybe the first book I write will be about her. I will call it, *Clarisse: Ravings of a Royal*, A Memoir, by Princess Mia of Genovia. And Grandmère won't be able to sue, just like Daryl Hannah couldn't sue when they made that movie about her and John F. Kennedy Junior, because all of it will be one hundred per cent true. HA! 'What DO you want for your birthday, Amelia?' Grandmère asked.

I had to think about that one. Of course, what I REALLY want Grandmère can't give me. But I figured it wouldn't hurt to ask. So I drew up the following list:

What I would like for my 15th birthday
by
Mia Thermopolis, aged 14 and 364 days

1. End to world hunger
2. New pair overalls, size eleven
3. New cat brush for Fat Louie (he chewed the handle off the last one)
4. Bungee cords for palace ballroom (so I can do air ballet like Lara Croft in *Tomb Raider*)
5. New baby brother or sister, safely delivered
6. Elevation of orcas to endangered list so Puget Sound can receive federal aid to clean up polluted breeding/feeding grounds
7. Lana Weinberger's head on a silver platter (just kidding – well, not really)
8. My own mobile phone
9. Grandmère to quit smoking
10. Michael Moscovitz to ask me to the Senior Prom

In composing this list, it occurred to me that sadly the only thing on it that I am likely to get for my birthday is item number 2. I mean, I *am* going to get a new brother or sister, but not for another month, at the earliest. No way was Grandmère going to go for the quitting smoking thing or the bungee cords. World hunger and the orca thing are sort of out of the hands of anyone I know. My dad says I would just lose and/or destroy a mobile, like I did the laptop he got me (that wasn't my fault. I only took it out of my backpack and set it on that sink for a second while I was looking for my Chapstick. It is not my fault that Lana Weinberger bumped into me and that the sinks at our school are all stopped up. That computer was only underwater for a few seconds — it fully should have worked again when it dried out. Except that even Michael, who is a technological as well as musical genius, couldn't save it).

Of course the one thing Grandmère fixated on was the last one, the one I only admitted to her in a moment of weakness and should never have mentioned in the first place, considering the fact that in twenty-four hours she and Michael will be sharing a table at Les Hautes Manger for my birthday dinner.

'What is the prom?' Grandmère wanted to know. 'I don't know this word.'

I couldn't believe it. But then Grandmère hardly ever watches TV, not even *Murder She Wrote* or *Golden Girls* reruns, like everyone else her age, so it was unlikely she'd ever have caught an airing of *Pretty in Pink* on TBS or whatever.

'It's a dance, Grandmère,' I said, reaching for my list. 'Never mind.'

'And the Moscovitz boy hasn't asked you to this dance yet?' Grandmère wanted to know. 'When is it?'

'A week from Saturday,' I said. 'Can I have that list back now?'

'Why don't you go without him?' Grandmère demanded. She let out a cackle, then seemed to think better of it, since I think it hurt her face to stretch her cheek muscles like that. 'Like you did last time. That'll show him.'

'I can't,' I said. 'It's only for seniors. I mean, seniors can take underclassmen, but underclassmen can't go on their own. Lilly says I should just ask Michael whether or not he's going, but—'

'NO!' Grandmère's eyes bulged. At first I thought she was choking on an ice cube, but it turned out she was just shocked. Grandmère's got eyeliner tattooed all the way around her lids like Michael Jackson, so she doesn't have to mess with her make-up every morning. So when her eyes bulge, well, it's pretty noticeable.

'You cannot *ask him*,' Grandmère said. 'How many

times do I have to tell you, Amelia? Men are like little woodland creatures. You have to *lure* them to you with tiny breadcrumbs and soft words of encouragement. You cannot simply whip out a rock and conk them over the head with it.'

I certainly agree with this. I don't want to do any conking where Michael is concerned. But I don't know about bread-crumbs.

'Well,' I said. 'So what do I do? The prom is in less than two weeks, Grandmère. If I'm going to go, I've got to know soon.'

'You must hint around the subject,' Grandmère said. '*Subtly.*'

I thought about this. 'Like do you mean I should go, "I saw the most perfect dress for the prom the other day in the Victoria's Secret catalogue?"'

'Exactly,' Grandmère said. 'Only of course a princess never purchases anything off the rack, Amelia, and NEVER from a catalogue.'

'Right,' I said. 'But, Grandmère, don't you think he'll see right through that?'

Grandmère snorted, then seemed to regret it, and held her drink up to her face, as if the ice in the glass was soothing to her tender skin. 'You are talking about a seventeen-year-old boy, Amelia,' she said. 'Not a master spy. He won't have the slightest idea what you are about, if you do it subtly enough.'

But I don't know. I mean, I have never been very good at being subtle. Like the other day I tried subtly to mention to my mother that Ronnie, our neighbour who Mom trapped in the hallway on the way to the incinerator room, might not have wanted to hear about how many times my mom has to get up and pee every night now that the baby is pressing so hard against her bladder. My mom just looked at me and went, 'Do you have a death wish, Mia?'

Mr Gianini and I have decided that we will be very relieved when my mom finally has this baby.

I am pretty sure Ronnie would agree.

Thursday, May 1, 12:01 a.m.

Well. That's it. I'm fifteen now. Not a girl. Not yet a woman.

Just like Britney.

HA HA HA.

I don't actually feel any different than I did a minute ago, when I was fourteen. I certainly don't LOOK any different. I'm the same five foot nine, thirty-two-A-bra-size freak I was when I turned fourteen. Maybe my hair looks a little better, since Grandmère made me get highlights and Paolo's been trimming it as it grows out. It is almost to my chin now, and not so triangular shaped as before.

Other than that, I'm sorry, but there's nothing. Nada. No difference. Zilch.

I guess all of my fifteeness is going to have to be on the inside, since it sure isn't showing on the outside.

I just checked my email to see if anybody remembered, and I already have five birthday messages, one from Lilly, one from Tina, one from my cousin Hank (I can't believe HE remembered. He's a famous model now and I almost never see him any more — no big loss — except half naked on billboards or the sides of telephone booths, which is especially embarrassing if he's wearing tighty-whities), one from my cousin Prince René and one from Michael.

41

The one from Michael is the best. It's a cartoon he's made himself, of a girl in a tiara with a big orange cat opening a giant present. When she gets all the wrapping off, these words burst out of the box, with all these fireworks: HAPPY BIRTHDAY, MIA, and in smaller letters, Love, Michael.

Love. LOVE!!!!!!!!!!!

Even though we have been going out for more than four months, I still get a thrill when he says — or writes — that word. In reference to me, I mean. Love. LOVE!!!!! He LOVES me!!!!!

So what's taking him so long about the prom thing, I'd like to know?

Now that I am fifteen, it is time that I put away childish things, like the guy in the poem, and begin to live my life as the adult that I am striving to become. According to Carl Jung, the famous psychoanalyst, in order to achieve *self-actualization — acceptance, peace, contentment, purposefulness, fulfilment, health, happiness and joy* — one must practise *compassion, love, charity, warmth, forgiveness, friendship, kindness, gratitude and trust.* Therefore, from now on, I pledge to:

1. Stop biting my nails. I really mean it this time
2. Make decent grades
3. Be nicer to people, even Lana Weinberger

4.   Write faithfully in my journal every day
5.   Start – and finish – a novel. Write one, I mean, not read one
6.   Get it published before I turn 20
7.   Be more understanding of Mom and what she is going through now that she is in the last trimester of her pregnancy
8.   Stop using Mr G's face-razor on my legs. Buy my own razors
9.   Try to be more sympathetic to Dad's abandonment issues while also getting out of having to spend July and August in Genovia
10. Figure out a way to get Michael Moscovitz to take me to the prom without stooping to trickery and/or grovelling

Once I've done all this, I should become fully self-actualized and ready to experience some well-deserved joy. And really, everything on that list is fairly doable. I mean, yes, it took Margaret Mitchell ten years to write *Gone With the Wind*, but I am only fifteen, so even if it takes me ten years to finish my own novel, I will still only be twenty-five by the time I get it published, which is only five years behind schedule.

The only problem is I don't really know what I'm going to write a novel about. But I'm sure I'll think of something soon. Maybe I should start practising with some short stories or haikus or something.

The prom thing, though. THAT is going to be hard. Because I truly do not want Michael to feel pressured about this. But I have GOT TO GO TO THE PROM!!! IT IS MY LAST CHANCE!!!!!!!

I hope Tina is right, and that Michael intends to ask me tonight at dinner.

OH PLEASE GOD LET TINA BE RIGHT!!!!!!!!!

Thursday, May 1, MY BIRTHDAY, Algebra

Josh asked Lana to the prom.

He asked her last night, after the varsity lacrosse game. The Lions won. According to Shameeka, who hung around after the junior varsity game, at which she'd cheered, Josh scored the winning goal. Then, as all the Albert Einstein fans poured out on to the field, Josh whipped off his shirt and swung it around in the air a few times, à la Mia Hamm, only of course Josh wasn't wearing a sports bra underneath. Shameeka says she was astounded by the lack of hair on Josh's chest. She said he was in no way Hugh Jackman-like in the goody trail department.

This, like the trouble my mother is currently having with her bladder, is really more than I want to know.

Anyway, Lana was on the sidelines, in her little sleeveless blue-and-gold AEHS cheerleading micro-mini. When Josh whipped his shirt off, she went running out on to the field, whooping. Then she leaped into his arms — which, considering that he was probably all sweaty, was a pretty risky endeavour, if you ask me — and they Frenched until Principal Gupta came over and whacked Josh on the back of the head with her clipboard. Then Shameeka says that Josh put Lana down and said, 'Go to the prom with me, babe?'

And Lana said yes, and then ran squealing over to all her fellow cheerleaders to tell them.

And I know that one of my resolutions now that I am fifteen is that I am going to be nicer to people, including Lana, but really, I am having a hard time right now keeping myself from stabbing my pencil into the back of her head. Well, not really, because I don't believe violence ever solves anything. Well, except for when it comes to getting rid of Nazis and terrorists and all. But, really, Lana is practically GLOATING. Before class started, she was fully on her mobile, telling everyone. Her mother is taking her to the Nicole Miller store in SoHo on Saturday to buy her a dress.

A black, off-one-shoulder dress, with a butterfly hem and a slit up one side. She's getting high heels that lace up the ankles, too, at Saks.

No doubt body glitter as well.

And I know I have a lot to feel grateful for. I mean, I have:

1. A super, loving boyfriend who, when the royal limo pulled over to pick him and Lilly up on the way to school today, presented me with a box of cinnamon mini-muffins, my favourites, from the Manhattan Muffin Company, which he'd gone all the way down to Tribeca really early in the morning to get me, in honour of my birthday.

2. An excellent best friend, who gave me a bright-pink cat collar for Fat Louie with the words *I Belong to Princess Mia* written on it in rhinestones that she'd hot-glue gunned on herself while watching old *Buffy the Vampire Slayer* reruns.

3. A great mom who, even if she does talk a little too much lately about her bodily functions, nevertheless dragged herself out of bed this morning to wish me a happy birthday.

4. A great stepdad who swore he wouldn't say anything in class about my birthday and embarrass me in front of everyone.

5. A dad who will probably give me something good for my birthday when I see him at dinner tonight, and a grandmother who, if she won't actually give me something I like, will at least WANT me to like it, whatever heinous thing it ends up being.

I seriously don't mean to be ungrateful for all of that, because it is so much more than so many people have. I mean, like kids in Appalachia — they are happy if they get socks for their birthday, or whatever, since their parents spend all their money on hooch.

But HELLO. IS IT TOO MUCH TO ASK THAT I GET THE ONE THING FOR MY BIRTHDAY THAT I HAVE ALWAYS

WANTED – and that is ONE PERFECT NIGHT AT THE PROM??????????????? I mean, Lana Weinberger is getting that, and she is not even striving to become self-actualized. She probably doesn't even know what self-actualization *means*. She has never been kind to anyone in her whole entire life. So why does SHE get to go to the prom?

I am telling you, there is no justice in the world.

NONE.

Expressions with radicals can be multiplied or divided as long as the root power or value under the radical is the same.

48

Thursday. May 1. MY BIRTHDAY. Gifted and Talented

Today, in honour of my birthday, Michael ate lunch at my table, instead of with the Computer Club, even though it's a Thursday. It was actually quite romantic, because it turns out that not only had he paid that little visit to the Manhattan Muffin Company this morning, but he also ditched fourth period and snuck out to Wu Liang Ye to get me the cold sesame noodles I like so much and can't get downtown, the ones that are so spicy you need to drink TWO cans of Coke before your tongue feels normal again after you eat them.

Which was totally sweet of him, and was actually even a bit of a relief, because I have been quite worried about what Michael is going to give me as a birthday present, because I know he must feel like he has a lot to live up to, seeing as how I got him a moon rock for his birthday.

I hope he realizes that, being a princess and all, I have access to moon rocks, but that I truly do not expect people to give me gifts that are of moon rock quality. I mean, I hope Michael knows that I would be happy with a simple, 'Mia, will you go to the prom with me?' And, of course, a Tiffany's charm bracelet with a charm that says *Property of Michael Moscovitz* on it that I could wear everywhere I go and so the next time some European prince asks me to dance at a ball I can hold up the bracelet and be all, 'Sorry, can't you read? I belong to Michael Moscovitz.'

Except Tina says even though it would be totally great if Michael got this for me, she doesn't think he will, because giving a girl – even his girlfriend – a chain that says *Property of Michael Moscovitz* seems a little presumptuous and not something Michael would do. I showed Tina the collar Lilly had given me for Fat Louie, but Tina says that isn't the same thing.

Is it wrong of me to want to be my boyfriend's property? I mean, it's not like I'm willing to usurp my own identity or take his name or anything if we got married (being a princess, even if I wanted to, I couldn't, unless I abdicated). In fact, chances are, the guy I marry is going to have to take MY name.

I just, you know, wouldn't mind a LITTLE possessiveness.

Uh-oh, something is going on. Michael just got up and went to the door to make sure Mrs Hill was firmly ensconced in the Teachers' Lounge, and Boris just came out of the supply closet, but the bell hasn't rung yet. What's up with that?

Thursday, May 1, still MY BIRTHDAY. French

I guess I needn't have worried about what Michael was going to get me for my birthday, because just now his band showed up — yes, his band, Skinner Box, right here in the G and T room. Well, Boris was already here because he is supposed to practise his violin during G and T, but the other band members — Felix, the drummer with the goatee, tall Paul the keyboardist and Trevor the guitar-player — all cut class to set up in the G and T classroom and play me a song Michael wrote just for me. It went:

> Combat boots and veggie burgers
> Just one glance gives me the shivers
> There she goes
> Princess of my heart

> Hates social injustice and nicotine
> She's no ordinary beauty queen
> There she goes
> Princess of my heart

Chorus: *Princess of my heart*
Oh I don't know where to start
Say I'll be your prince
Till this lifetime ends.

Princess of my heart
I loved you from the start
Say you love me too
Over my heart you so rule.

Promise you won't execute me
with those gorgeous smiles you shoot me
There she goes
Princess of my heart

You don't even have to knight me
Every time you laugh you smite me
There she goes
Princess of my heart

Chorus: *Princess of my heart*
Oh I don't know where to start
Say I'll be your prince
Till this lifetime ends.

52

Princess of my heart
I loved you from the start
Say you love me too
and then together we will rule.

And this time there was no question the song was about me, like there was that time Michael played me that 'Tall Drink of Water' song he wrote!

Anyway, the whole school heard Michael's song about me because Skinner Box had their amps turned up so loud. Mrs Hill and everybody else who was in the Teachers' Lounge came out of it, waited politely for Skinner Box to finish the song, then gave the whole band detention.

And, OK, on Mademoiselle Klein's birthday, Mr Wheeton had a dozen red roses delivered to her in the middle of fifth period. But he didn't write a song just for her and play it for the whole school to hear.

And, yeah, Lana may be going to the prom, but her boyfriend – not to mention his friends – never got detention for her.

So really, except for the whole having-to-spend-July-and-August-in-Genovia thing – oh, and the prom thing – fifteen is looking pretty good so far.

Homework:

Algebra: You would think my own stepfather would be
  nice and not give me homework on MY BIRTHDAY,
  but no

English: *The Iceman Cometh*

Biology: Ice worm

Health and Safety: Check with Lilly

Gifted and Talented: As if

French: Check with Tina

World Civ.: God knows

Thursday, May 1, still MY BIRTHDAY, the ladies' room at Les Hautes Manger

OK, this is so my best birthday ever.

I am serious. I mean, even my mom and dad are getting along with each other — or trying to, anyway. It is so sweet. I am so proud of them. You can totally tell my mom's maternity tights are driving her crazy, but she isn't complaining about them a bit, and Dad totally hasn't said anything about the anarchy symbols she's wearing as earrings. And Mr Gianini put Grandmère right off her lecture about his goatee (Grandmère cannot abide facial hair on a man) by telling her that she looks younger and younger every time he sees her. Which you could tell pleased Grandmère no end, since she was smiling all through the appetizers (she can move her lips again now that the inflammation from her chemical peel has finally died down).

I was a little worried that Mr G's observation would cause my mom to go off on the beauty industry and how they are ageist and are constantly trying to propagate the myth that you can't be attractive unless you have the dewy skin of someone my age (which doesn't even make sense since most people my age have zits unless they can afford a fancy dermatologist like the one Grandmère sends me to, who gives me all these prescription unguents so that I can avoid unprincesslike breakouts), but she totally refrained in my honour.

And when Michael showed up late on account of having been in detention, Grandmère didn't say anything mean about it, which was such a relief, because Michael looked kind of flushed, as if he'd run the whole way from his apartment after he'd gone home to change. I guess even Grandmère could tell he'd really tried to be on time.

And even someone who is totally immune to normal human emotion like Grandmère would have to admit that my boyfriend was the handsomest guy in the whole restaurant. Michael's dark hair was sort of flopping over one eye, and he looked SO cute in his non-school-uniform jacket and tie, which is part of the mandatory dress code at Les Hautes Manger (I warned him ahead of time).

Anyway, Michael's showing up was kind of the signal I guess for everyone to start handing me the presents they'd got me.

And what presents! I am telling you, I cleaned up. Being fifteen RULES!

DAD

OK, so Dad got me a very fancy and expensive-feeling pen — to use, he said, to further my writing career (I am using it to write this very journal entry). Of course I would have rather had a season pass to Six Flags Great Adventure theme park for the summer (and permission to stay in this country to use it) but the pen is very nice, all purple and gold, and has *HRH Princess Amelia Renaldo* engraved on it.

MOM and MR G

A mobile phone!!!!!!!!!!!! Yes!!!!!!!!! Of my very own!!!!!!!!!

Sadly the mobile phone was accompanied by a lecture from Mom and Mr G about how they'd only bought it for me so that they can reach me when my mom goes into labour, since she wants me to be in the room (this is so not going to happen due to my excessive dislike of seeing anything spurt out of anything else, but you don't argue with a woman who has to pee twenty-four hours a day) while my baby brother or sister is born, and how I'm not to use the phone during school and how it is a domestic-use-only calling policy, nothing transatlantic, so when I am in Genovia don't think I can call Michael on it.

But I didn't pay any attention, because YAY! I actually got something on my list!!!!!

GRANDMÈRE

OK, this is very weird because Grandmère actually gave me something else from my list. Only it wasn't bungee cords, a cat brush or new overalls. It was a letter declaring me the official sponsor of a real live African orphan named Johanna!!!!!!! Grandmère said, 'I can't help you end world hunger, but I suppose I can help you send one little girl to bed every night with a good dinner.'

I was so surprised, I nearly blurted out, 'But, Grandmère! You hate poor people!' because it's true, she totally does. Whenever she sees those runaway teen punk rockers who sit outside Lincoln Center in their leather jackets and Doc Martens, with those signs that say *Homeless and Hungry*, she always snaps at them, 'If you'd stop spending all your money on tattoos and naval rings, you'd be able to afford a nice sublet in NoLita!'

But I guess Johanna is a different story, seeing as how she doesn't have parents back in Westchester who are sick with worry about her.

I don't know what is going on with Grandmère. I fully expected her to give me a mink stole or something equally revolting for my birthday. But getting me something I actually *wanted* . . . helping me to sponsor a starving orphan . . . that is almost *thoughtful* of her. I must say, I am still in a bit of shock over the whole thing.

I think my mom and dad feel the same way. My dad ordered up a Martini after he saw what Grandmère had given me, and my mom just sat there in total silence for like the first time since she got pregnant. I am not kidding, either.

Then Lars gave me his gift, even though it is not correct Genovian protocol to receive gifts from one's bodyguard (because look what happened to Princess Stephanie of Monaco: her bodyguard gave her a birthday present, and she MARRIED him. Which would have been all right if they'd had anything in common, but Stephanie's bodyguard isn't the least bit interested in eyebrow threading, and Stephanie clearly knows nothing about ju-jitsu, so the whole thing was off to a rocky start to begin with).

Anyway, you could tell Lars had really put a lot of thought into his gift, because it was:

LARS

An authentic New York Police Department Bomb Squad baseball cap, which Lars got from an actual NYPD bomb squad officer once when he was sweeping Grandmère's suite at the Plaza for incendiary devices prior to a visit from the Pope. Which I thought was SO sweet of Lars, because I know how much he treasured that hat, and the fact that he was willing to give it to me is true proof of his devotion, which I highly doubt is of the matrimonial variety, since I happen to know Lars loves Mademoiselle Klein, like all heterosexual men who come within seven feet of her.

But the best present of all was the one from Michael. He didn't give it to me in front of everybody else. He waited until I got up to go to the bathroom just now, and followed me. Then just as I was starting down the stairs to the ladies' he went, 'Mia, this is for you. Happy birthday,' and gave me this flat little box all wrapped up in gold foil.

I was really surprised – almost as surprised as I'd been over Grandmère's gift. I was all, 'Michael, but you already gave me a present! You wrote that song for me! You got detention for me!'

But Michael just went, 'Oh, that. That wasn't your present. This is.'

And, I have to admit, the box was little and flat enough that I thought – I really did think – it might have prom tickets in it. I thought maybe, I don't know, that Lilly had told Michael how much I wanted to go to the prom, and that he'd gone and bought the tickets to surprise me.

Well, he surprised me, all right. Because what was in the box wasn't prom tickets.

But, still, it was almost as good.

MICHAEL

A necklace with a tiny little silver snowflake hanging from it.

'From when we were at the Non-denominational Winter

Dance,' he said, like he was worried I wouldn't get it. 'Remember the paper snowflakes hanging from the ceiling of the gym?'

Of course I remembered the snowflakes. I had one in the drawer of my bedside table.

And, OK, it isn't a prom ticket or a charm with *Property of Michael Moscovitz* written on it, but it comes really, really close.

So I gave Michael a great big kiss right there by the stairs to the ladies' room, in front of all the Les Hautes Manger waiters and the hostess and the coat-check girl and everyone. I didn't care who saw. For all I care, *US Weekly* could have snapped all the shots of us they wanted — even run them on the front cover of next week's edition with a caption that says *Mia Makes Out!* — and I wouldn't have blinked an eye. That's how happy I was.

Am. That's how happy I *am*. My fingers are trembling as I write this, because I think, for the first time in my life, it is possible that I have finally, finally reached the upper branches of the Jungian tree of self-actual—

Wait a minute. There is a lot of noise coming from the hallway. Like breaking dishes and a dog barking and someone screaming . . .

Oh my God. That's *Grandmère* screaming.

Friday, May 2, midnight, the Loft

I should have known it was too good to be true. My birthday, I mean. It was all just going too well. I mean, no prom invitation or cancellation of my trip to Genovia, but, you know, everyone I love (well, almost everyone) sitting at one table, not fighting. Getting everything I wanted (well, almost everything). Michael writing that song about me. And the snowflake necklace. And the mobile phone.

Oh, but wait. This is ME we're talking about. I think that, at fifteen, it's time I admitted what I've known for quite some time now: I am simply not destined to have a normal life. Not a normal life, not a normal family and certainly not a normal birthday.

Granted, this one might have been the exception, if it hadn't been for Grandmère. Grandmère and Rommel.

I ask you, who brings a DOG to a RESTAURANT? I don't care if it's normal in France. NOT SHAVING UNDER YOUR ARMS IF YOU ARE A GIRL IS NORMAL IN FRANCE. Does that maybe TELL you something about France? I mean, for God's sake, they eat SNAILS there. SNAILS. Who in their right mind thinks that if something is normal in France it is at all socially acceptable here in the US?

I'll tell you who. My grandmother, that's who.

Seriously. She doesn't understand what the fuss is about. She's all, 'But of course I brought Rommel.'

To Les Hautes Manger. To my birthday dinner. My grandmother brought her DOG to MY BIRTHDAY DINNER.

She says it's only because when she leaves Rommel alone he licks himself until his hair falls out. It is an Obsessive Compulsive Disorder diagnosed by the Royal Genovian vet, and Rommel has prescription medication he is supposed to take to help keep it at bay.

That's right: my grandmother's dog is on Prozac.

But, if you ask me, I don't think OCD is Rommel's problem. Rommel's problem is that he lives with Grandmère. If *I* had to live with Grandmère, I would totally lick off all my hair. If my tongue were long enough, anyway.

Still, just because her dog suffers from OCD is NO excuse for Grandmère to bring him to MY BIRTHDAY dinner. In a Hermes handbag. With a broken clasp, no less.

Because what happened while I was in the ladies' room? Oh, Rommel escaped from Grandmère's handbag. And started streaking around the restaurant, desperate to evade capture – as who under Grandmère's tyrannical rule wouldn't?

I can only imagine what the patrons of Les Hautes Manger must have thought, seeing this eight-pound hairless miniature poodle zipping in and out from beneath the tablecloths. Actually, I know what they thought. I know what they thought, because Michael told me later. They thought Rommel was a giant rat.

And it's true without hair he does have a very rodent-like appearance.

But, still, I don't think climbing up on to their chairs and shrieking their heads off was necessarily the most helpful thing to do about it. Although Michael did say a number of the tourists whipped out digital cameras and started shooting away. I am sure there is going to be a headline in some Japanese newspaper tomorrow about the giant rat problem of the Manhattan four-star restaurant scene.

Anyway, I didn't see what happened next, but Michael told me it was just like in a Baz Luhrmann movie, only Nicole Kidman was nowhere to be seen: this busboy who apparently hadn't noticed the ruckus came hustling by, holding this enormous tray of half-empty soup bowls. Suddenly Rommel, who'd almost been cornered by my dad over by the seafood bar, darted into the busboy's path, and the next thing everyone knew, lobster bisque was flying everywhere.

Thankfully, most of it landed on Grandmère. The lobster bisque, I mean. She fully deserved to have her Chanel suit ruined on account of being stupid enough to bring her DOG to MY BIRTHDAY dinner. I so wish I had seen this.

No one would admit it later — not even Mom — but I bet it was really, really, really funny to see Grandmère covered in soup. I swear, if that's all I had got for my birthday, I'd have been totally happy.

But by the time I got out of the bathroom, Grandmère had been thoroughly dabbed by the maître d'. All you could see of the soup were these wet parts all over her chest. I completely missed out on all the fun (as usual). Instead, I got there just in time to see the maître d' imperiously ordering the poor busboy to turn in his dish towel: he was fired.

FIRED!!! And for something that was fully not his fault!

Jangbu — that was the busboy's name — totally looked as if he were going to cry. He kept saying over and over again how sorry he was. But it didn't matter. Because if you spill soup on a dowager princess in New York City, you can kiss your career in the restaurant biz goodbye. It would be like if a gourmet cook got caught going to McDonald's in Paris. Or if P. Diddy got caught buying underwear at Wal-Mart. Or if Nicky and Paris Hilton got caught lying around in their Juicy Couture sweats on a Saturday night, watching *National Geographic Explorer*, instead of going out to party. It is simply Not Done.

I tried to reason with the maître d' on Jangbu's behalf, after Michael told me what had happened. I said in no way could Grandmère hold the restaurant responsible for what HER dog had done. A dog she wasn't even supposed to have HAD in the restaurant in the first place.

But it didn't do any good. The last I saw of Jangbu, he was heading sadly back towards the kitchen.

I tried to get Grandmère, who was, after all, the injured party – or the allegedly injured party, since of course she wasn't in the least bit hurt – to talk the maître d'into giving Jangbu his job back. But she remained stubbornly unmoved by my pleas on Jangbu's behalf. Even my reminding her that many busboys are immigrants, new to this country, with families to support back in their native lands, left her cold.

'Grandmère,' I cried in desperation. 'What makes Jangbu so different from Johanna, the African orphan you are sponsoring on my behalf ? Both are merely trying to make their way on this planet we call Earth.'

'The difference between Johanna and Jangbu,' Grandmère informed me, as she held Rommel close, trying to calm him down (it took the combined efforts of Michael, my dad, Mr G and Lars to finally catch Rommel, right before he made a run for it through the revolving door and out on to Fifth Avenue and freedom on the miniature-poodle underground railroad), 'is that Johanna did not SPILL SOUP ALL OVER ME!'

God. She is such a CRAB sometimes.

So now here I am, knowing that somewhere in the city —
Queens, most likely — is a young man whose family will
probably starve, and all because of MY BIRTHDAY. That's
right. Jangbu lost his job because I WAS BORN.

I'm sure wherever Jangbu is right now, he is wishing I
wasn't. Born, that is.

And I can't say that I blame him one little bit.

Friday, May 2, 1 a.m., the Loft

My snowflake necklace is really nice, though. I am never, ever taking it off.

Friday, May 2, 1:05 a.m., the Loft

Well, except maybe when I go swimming. Because I wouldn't want it to get lost.

Friday, May 2, 1:10 a.m., the Loft

He loves me!

Friday, May 2, Algebra

Oh my God. It is all over the city. About Grandmère and the incident at Les Hautes Manger last night, I mean. It must be a slow news day, because even the *Post* picked it up. It was right there on the front cover at the news-stand on the corner:

A Royal Mess, screams *The Post*.

Princess and the Pea (Soup), claims the *Daily News* (erroneously, since it wasn't pea soup at all, but lobster bisque).

It even made *The Times*! You would think that *The New York Times* would be above reporting something like that, but there it was, in the Metro section. Lilly pointed it out as she climbed into the limo with Michael this morning.

'Well, your grandmother's certainly done it this time,' Lilly says.

As if I didn't already know it! As if I wasn't already suffering from the crippling guilt of knowing that I was, even in an indirect manner, to blame for Jangbu's loss of livelihood!

Although I do have to admit that I was somewhat distracted from my grief over Jangbu by the fact that Michael looked so incredibly hot, as he does every morning when he gets into my limo. That is because when we come to pick him and Lilly up for school, Michael has always just shaved, and his face is looking all smooth. Michael is not a particularly hairy person but it is true that by the end of the day — which is when we usually end up doing our kissing, since we are both somewhat shy people, I think, and we have the cover of darkness to hide our burning cheeks — Michael's facial hair has gotten a bit on the sandpapery side. In fact, I can't help thinking that it would be much nicer to kiss Michael in the morning, when his face is all smooth, than at night, when it is all scratchy. Especially his neck. Not that I have ever thought about kissing my boyfriend's neck. I mean, that would just be weird.

Although, as far as boys' necks go, Michael has a very nice one. Sometimes on the rare occasions when we are actually alone long enough to start making out, I put my nose next to Michael's neck and just inhale. I know it sounds strange, but Michael's neck smells really, really nice, like soap. Soap and something else. Something that makes me feel like nothing bad could ever happen to me, not when I am in Michael's arms, smelling his neck.

IF ONLY HE WOULD ASK ME TO THE PROM!!!!!!!!!! Then I could spend a whole NIGHT smelling his neck, only it would look like we were dancing, so no one, not even Michael, would know.

Wait a minute. What was I saying before I got distracted by the smell of my boyfriend's neck?

Oh yes. Grandmère. Grandmère and Jangbu.

Anyway, none of the newspaper articles about what happened last night mention the part about Rommel. Not one. There is not even a hint of a suggestion that the whole thing might possibly have been Grandmère's own fault. Oh no! Not at all!

But Lilly knows about it, on account of Michael having told her. And she had a lot to say about it.

'What we'll do,' she said, 'is we'll start making signs in Gifted and Talented class, and then we'll go over after school.'

'Go over where?' I wanted to know. I was still busy staring at Michael's smooth neck.

'To Les Hautes Manger,' Lilly said. 'To start the protest.'

'What protest?' All I seemed to be able to think about was whether my neck smells as good to Michael as his does to me. To tell the truth, I cannot even remember a time when Michael might have smelt my neck. Since he is taller than me, it is very easy for me to put my nose up to his neck and smell it. But for him to smell mine he would have to lean down, which might look a bit weird, and could conceivably cause whiplash.

'The protest against their unfair dismissal of Jangbu

Pinasa!' Lilly shouted. Great. So now I know what I am doing after school. Like I don't have enough problems, what with:

a) My princess lessons with Grandmère
b) Homework
c) Worrying about the party Mom is having for me Saturday night and the fact that probably no one will show up and even if they *do* it is entirely possible that my mom and Mr G might *do* something to embarrass me in front of them, such as complain about their bodily functions or possibly start playing the drums
d) Next week's menu for *The Atom* being due
e) The fact that my father expects me to spend sixty-two days with him in *Genovia* this summer
f) My boyfriend still not having asked me to the prom

Oh no, let me just FORGET ALL ABOUT all THAT stuff and worry about Jangbu.

I mean, don't get me wrong, I am totally worried about him, but, hello, I have my own problems too. Like the fact that Mr G just passed back the quizzes from Monday, and mine has a big red C minus on it and a note: *SEE ME*.

Um, hello, Mr G, like I didn't just see you AT BREAKFAST. You couldn't have mentioned this THEN?

Oh my God, Lana just turned round and slapped a copy of *New York Newsday* on my desk. There is a huge picture on the cover of Grandmère leaving Les Hautes Manger with Rommel cowering in her arms, and bits of lobster bisque still stuck to her skirt.

'Why is your family so full of FREAKS?' Lana wants to know.

You know what, Lana? That is a very good question.

Friday, May 2, Bio

I cannot believe Mr G. The *nerve* of him, suggesting that my relationship with Michael is DISTRACTING me from my schoolwork! As if Michael has ever done anything but try to help me to understand Algebra. Hello!

And, OK, so Michael comes in to visit me every morning before class starts. So what? How is that harming anyone? I mean, yeah, it makes LANA mad, because Josh Richter NEVER comes in to see HER before class, because he is too busy admiring his own highlights in the men's room mirror. But how is THAT distracting me from my schoolwork?

I am going to have to have a serious talk with my mother, because I think the impending birth of his first child is turning Mr G into a misanthrope. So what if I got a sixty-nine on the last quiz? A person can have an off day, can't she? That does NOT mean that my grades are slipping, or that I am spending too much time with Michael, or thinking about smelling his neck every waking moment of the day, or anything like that.

And Mr G suggesting that I spent the entirety of second period this morning writing in my journal is completely laughable. I fully paid attention to his little lecture about the polynomials towards the last ten minutes or so of class. PLEASE!

And that thing where I wrote HRH Michael Moscovitz Renaldo seventeen times at the bottom of my worksheet was just a JOKE. God. Mr G, what happened to you? You *used* to have a sense of humour.

Friday. May 2. Bio

So . . . did he ask you last night? At your birthday dinner. S

No.

Mia! There are exactly nine days until the prom. You are going to have to take matters into your own hands and just ask him.

SHAMEEKA! You know I can't do that.

Well, it's getting to be crunch time. If he doesn't ask you by the party tomorrow night, you aren't going to be able to say yes if he DOES ask you. I mean, a girl has to have some pride.

That is very easy for someone like you to say, Shameeka. You are a cheerleader.

Yeah. And you're a princess!

You know what I mean.

Mia, you can't let him take you for granted in this way. You have to keep boys on

78

their toes . . . . no matter how many songs
they write for you, or snowflake necklaces
they give you. You've got to let them know
YOU'RE in charge.

    You sound just like my grandmother sometimes.

EEEEEEEEEEEWWWWWWWWWWWW!

Friday, May 2. Gifted and Talented

Oh my God, Lilly will NOT shut up about Jangbu and his plight. Look, I feel for the guy too, but I am not about to violate the poor man's privacy by trying to track down his home phone number — especially not using a certain royal's BRAND-SPANKING-NEW MOBILE PHONE.

I have not even been able to make ONE call from it. Not ONE. Lilly has already made five.

This busboy thing is totally out of control. Lesley Cho, the *Atom*'s editor-in-chief, stopped by our table at lunch and asked if I could do an in-depth story on the incident for Monday's paper. I realize that now at last I have been given my entrée into real reporting, and not just working the cafeteria beat, but does Lesley really think I am the most appropriate person for this job? I mean, isn't she running the risk of this story being less than completely prejudice-free and unbiased? Sure, I think Grandmère was wrong, but she's still my GRANDMOTHER, for crying out loud.

I am not sure I really appreciate this peek into the seedy underbelly of school newspaper reporting. Working on a novel instead of writing for the *Atom* is starting to look more and more appealing.

Since it is Friday and Michael was up at the bean bar getting me a second helping, and Lilly was otherwise occupied, Tina asked me what I am going to do about Michael's not having asked me to the prom yet.

'What CAN I do?' I wailed. 'I just have to sit around and wait, like Jane Eyre did when Mr Rochester was busy playing billiards with Blanche Ingram and pretending like he didn't know Jane was alive.'

To which Tina replied, 'I really think you should say something. Maybe tomorrow night, at your party?'

Oh, great. I was kind of looking forward to my party — you know, except for the part where Mom was sure to stop everyone at the door and tell them all about her Incredible Shrinking Bladder — but now? No chance. Because I know Tina will be staring at me all night, willing me to ask Michael about the prom. Great. Thanks.

Lilly just handed me this giant sign. It says, LES HAUTES MANGER IS UN-AMERICAN!

I pointed out to Lilly that everyone already knows Les Hautes Manger is un-American. It is a French restaurant. To which Lilly replied, 'Just because its owner was born in France is no reason for him to think he does not have to abide by our nation's laws and social customs.'

I said I thought it was one of our laws that people could

pretty much hire and fire who they wanted to. You know, within certain parameters.

'Just whose side are you on in this, anyway, Mia?' Lilly wanted to know.

I said, 'Yours, of course. I mean, Jangbu's.'

But doesn't Lilly realize I have way too many problems of my own to take on an itinerant busboy's as well? I mean, I have the summer to worry about, not to mention my Algebra grade, and an African orphan to support. And I really don't think I can be expected to help get Jangbu's job back when I can't even get my own boyfriend to ask me to the prom.

I gave Lilly her sign back, explaining that I won't be able to come to the protest after school, as I have a princess lesson to attend. Lilly accused me of being more concerned for myself than for Jangbu's three starving children. I asked her how she knew Jangbu even had kids, because so far as I knew this had not been mentioned in any of the newspaper articles about the incident, and Lilly still hadn't managed to get hold of him. But she just said she meant figuratively, not literally.

I am very concerned about Jangbu and his figurative children, it is true. But it is a dog-eat-dog world out there, and right now I've got problems of my own. I'm almost positive Jangbu would understand.

But I told Lilly I'd try to talk Grandmère into talking the owner of Les Hautes Manger into hiring Jangbu back. I guess it's the least I can do, considering my presence on earth is the reason the poor guy's livelihood was destroyed.

Homework:
Algebra: Who knows
English: Who cares
Biology: Whatever
Health and Safety: Please
Gifted and Talented: As if
French: Something
World Civ.: Something else

Friday, May 2, in the limo on the way home from Grandmère's

Grandmère has decided to act like nothing happened last night. Like she didn't bring her poodle to my birthday dinner and get an innocent busboy fired. Like her face wasn't plastered all over the front of every newspaper in Manhattan, minus *The Times*. She was just going on about how in Japan it is considered terrifically rude to poke your chopstick into your rice bowl. Apparently, if you do this, it is a sign of disrespect to the dead, or something.

Whatever. Like I am going to Japan any time soon. Hello, apparently I am not even going to my own PROM.

'Grandmère,' I said, when I couldn't take it any more. 'Are we going to talk about what happened at dinner last night, or are you just going to pretend like it didn't happen?'

Grandmère looked all innocent. 'I'm sorry, Amelia. I can't think what you mean.'

'Last night,' I said. 'My birthday dinner. At Les Hautes Manger. You got the busboy fired. It was all over the papers this morning.'

'Oh, that.' Grandmère innocently stirred her Sidecar.

'Well?' I asked her. 'What are you going to do about it?'

'Do?' Grandmère looked genuinely surprised. 'Why, nothing. What is there to do?'

I guess I shouldn't have been so shocked. Grandmère can be pretty self-absorbed, when she wants to be.

'Grandmère, a man lost his job because of you,' I cried. 'You've got to do something! He could starve.'

Grandmère looked at the ceiling. 'Good heavens, Amelia. I already got you an orphan. Are you saying you want to adopt a busboy, as well?'

'No. But, Grandmère, it wasn't Jangbu's fault that he spilt soup on you. It was an accident. But it was caused by your dog.'

Grandmère shielded Rommel's ears.

'Not so loud,' she said. 'He's very sensitive. The vet said—'

'I don't care what the vet said,' I yelled. 'Grandmère, you've got to do something! My friends are down at the restaurant picketing it right now!'

Just to be dramatic, I switched on the television and turned it to New York One. I didn't really expect there to be anything on it about Lilly's protest. Just maybe something about how there was a traffic snarl in the area, due to rubberneckers peering at the spectacle Lilly was making of herself.

So you can imagine I was pretty surprised when a second

later, a reporter started describing the 'extraordinary scene outside Les Hautes Manger, the trendy four-star eatery on Fifty-Seventh Street,' and they showed Lilly marching around with a big sign that said LES HAUTES MANGER MGMT UNFAIR. The biggest surprise wasn't the large number of Albert Einstein High School students Lilly had managed to talk into joining her. I mean, I expected to see Boris there, and it wasn't exactly astonishing to see that the AEHS Socialist Club was there as well, since they will show up to any protest they can find.

No, the big shocker was that there was a large number of men I'd never seen before marching right alongside Lilly and the other AEHS students.

The reporter soon explained why.

'Busboys from all over the city have gathered here in front of Les Hautes Manger to show their solidarity with Jangbu Pinasa, the employee who was dismissed from Les Hautes Manger last night after an incident involving the Dowager Princess of Genovia.'

In spite of all of this, however, Grandmère remained completely unmoved. She just looked at the screen and clacked her tongue.

'Blue,' she said, 'isn't Lilly's best colour, is it?'

I seriously don't know what I am going to do with the woman. She is completely IMPOSSIBLE.

Friday, May 2, the Loft

You would think in my own house I would find a little peace and quiet. But no, I come home to find my mom and Mr G in a raging fight. Usually their fights are about the fact that Mom wants a home birth with a midwife and Mr G wants a hospital birth with the staff of the Mayo Clinic in attendance.

But this time it was because my mom wants to name the baby Simone if it's a girl, after Simone de Beauvoir, and Sartre if it's a boy, after — well, some guy named Sartre, I guess.

But Mr G wants to name the baby Rose if it's a girl, after his grandma, and Rocky if it's a boy, after . . . well, apparently after Sylvester Stallone. Which, you know, having seen the movie *Rocky*, isn't necessarily a bad thing, since Rocky was very nice and all . . .

But my mom says over her dead body will her son — if she has a son — be named after a practically illiterate prizefighter.

Still, if you ask me, Rocky is better than the last name they came up with if it's a boy: Granger. Thank God I went and looked up Granger in the baby-name book I bought them. Because once I let them know that Granger means 'farmer' in Middle French, they totally cooled on it. Who names their baby Farmer?

Amelia doesn't mean anything in French. It is said to be derivative of Emily, or Emmeline, which means 'industrious' in Old German. The name Michael, which is old Hebrew, means 'He who is like the Lord'. So you see that, together, we make a very nice pair, being industrious and lord-like.

But the fight didn't end with the whole Sartre versus Rocky thing. Oh no. My mom wants to go to B.J.'s Wholesale Outlet in Jersey City tomorrow to buy the supplies for my party, but Mr G is scared terrorists might set off a bomb in the Holland Tunnel, trapping them in there like Sylvester Stallone in the movie *Daylight*, and then Mom might go into labour prematurely and have the baby with the water from the Hudson River gushing all around.

Mr G just wants to go to Paper House on Broadway to buy Queen Amidala birthday plates and cups.

Hello, I hope they know I am fifteen years, not months, old, and that I can perfectly understand everything that they are saying.

Whatever. I put on my headphones and turned on my computer in the hopes of finding some solace away from all the raised voices, but no such luck. Lilly could only have just got home from her protest thingy, but she's already managed to send around a mass email to everyone in school:

ATTENTION

ALL STUDENTS AT ALBERT EINSTEIN HIGH SCHOOL

Your help and support is vitally needed by the Students Against The Wrongful Dismissal Of Jangbu Pinasa Association (SATWDOJPA)! Join us tomorrow (Saturday, May 3) at noon for a rally in Central Park, and then a protest march down Fifth Avenue to the doors of Les Hautes Manger on 57th Street. Show your disapproval over the way New York City restaurateurs treat their employees! Do not listen to the people who argue that Generation Y is the Materialistic Generation! Make your voice heard!

Lilly Moscovitz, President

SATWDOJPA

Hello. I didn't know my generation was the Materialistic Generation. How can that even be? I hardly own anything. Except a mobile phone. And I've only had that for like a day.

There was another message from Lilly. It went:

Fr: WomynRule

Mia, missed you today at the rally. You should have been there, it was totally AMAZING! Busboys from as far away as Chinatown joined our peaceful protest. There was such a feeling of camaraderie and

warmth! Best of all, you'll never guess who showed up . . . Jangbu Pinasa himself! He came to Les Hautes Manger to pick up his last pay cheque. Was he ever surprised to see us all there, picketing on his behalf! He was really shy at first and didn't want to talk to me. But I informed him that, though I might have been brought up in an upper-class household, and my parents are members of the intelligentsia, at heart I am as working class as he is, and have only the best interests of the common man at heart. Jangbu is coming to the march tomorrow! You should come too – it's going to be awesome!!!!!!!!!
Lilly

PS You didn't tell me Jangbu was only eighteen years old. Did you know that he is a Sherpa? Seriously. From Tibet. Back in his home country, he already graduated from high school. He came here searching for a better life because agricultural trade in his homeland has been brought to a standstill by the politics of the Chinese occupying power, and the only non-agricultural job young Sherpas can get is serving as porters and guides in the Himalayas. But Jangbu doesn't like heights.
PPS You also didn't tell me he was so HOT!!!! He

looks like a cross between Jackie Chan and Enrique Inglesias. Only without the cheek mole.

It really is quite exhausting to have geniuses as both your best friend as well as your boyfriend. I swear I can hardly keep up with the two of them. Their mental gymnastics are totally beyond me.

Fortunately there was also an email from Tina, whose intellectual capacity is more equal to my own:

Iluvromance: Mia, I've been thinking it over, and I've decided that the best time for you to ask Michael whether or not he is going to ask you to the prom really will be tomorrow night at your party. What I think we should do is organize a game of Seven Minutes in Heaven. (Your mom won't care, right? I mean, she and Mr G aren't going to actually BE THERE during the party, are they?) And when you are in the closet with Michael, and things get hot and heavy with him, you should pop the question. Believe me, no boy can say no to anything during Seven Minutes in Heaven. Or so I've read.

Jeez! What is with my friends? It is like they live in a completely different universe from me. Seven Minutes in

Heaven? Has Tina lost her mind? I want to have a NICE party, with Coke and Cheetos and maybe the Time Warp if I can get Mr G to help me move the futon couch. I do NOT want a party where people are going off in the closet to make out. I mean, if I want to make out with my boyfriend, I will do it in the privacy of my own room . . . except of course that I'm not allowed to have Michael over when no one else is home, and when he is over I have to leave the bedroom door open at least four inches at all times (thanks, Mr G. You know, it totally sucks having a stepfather who is also a high-school teacher, because who is better equipped to rain on a teenager's parade than a high-school teacher?).

I swear, between my grandmother and my friends, I don't know who causes me the most headaches.

At least Michael left a nice message:

LinuxRulz: You seemed pretty quiet during G and T today. Are you OK?

Thank God my boyfriend can be counted on to always be supportive of me. Except, of course, when he neglects to ask me to the prom.

I decided to ignore Lilly's and Tina's emails, but I wrote back to Michael. I tried to implement some of that subtlety

Grandmère was talking about the other day. Not that I approve of Grandmère right now, or anything. Still, it must be stated that she has had a lot more boyfriends than I have.

FtLouie: Hey! I'm fine. Thanks for asking. I just can't shake this feeling lately that there's something I've forgotten. I can't quite put my finger on what it is, though. Something to do with this time of year, I think . . .

There! Perfect! Subtle, yet pointed. And Michael, being a genius, was sure to get it.

Or so I thought, until he wrote back . . . which he did right away, since I guess he was online as well.

LinuxRulz: Well, judging by the C you got on that quiz today, I'd say what you're forgetting is everything we've been going over these past few weeks in Algebra. If you want, I'll come over on Sunday and help you with Monday's assignment.

Oh my God. Did any girl ever have a boyfriend so totally clueless? Except possibly Lilly? Except that I think even Boris Pelkowski would have seen through my artless ploy.

I am so depressed. I think I am going to go to bed. There is a *Farscape* marathon on, but I am not in the mood to watch other people's space adventures. My own are upsetting enough.

Saturday, May 3, DAY OF THE BIG PARTY

My mom poked her head in bright and early and asked me if I wanted to go with her and Mr G to B.J.'s for party supplies. Normally I love B.J.'s, on account of the cavernous warehouse filled with oversize stuff, and the free cheese samples and the popcorn and everything. Not to mention the drive-through liquor store Mr G likes to hit on the way home, where they open your boot and fill it with six-packs of Coke without your ever even having to get out of the car.

But for some reason today I was too depressed even for the drive-through liquor store. So I just stayed under the covers and asked my mom weakly if she minded going by herself. I said I had a sore throat and thought I should stay in bed until it was time for the party, just to make sure I was well enough actually to attend it.

I don't think my mom really fell for the whole sick act, but she didn't say anything about it. She just went, 'Suit yourself,' and left with Mr G. Which, considering the mood she's been in lately, is actually letting me off pretty lightly.

I don't know what's wrong with me. I am such a failure. I mean, I have all these problems. I want to go to the prom with my boyfriend, only he hasn't asked me, and I'm too afraid he'll think I'm being pushy to discuss it with him. I

95

don't want to spend my summer in Genovia, but I signed a stinking contract saying I would, and now I don't think I can get out of it. My best friend is trying to do all this good for mankind and everything, and I can't be bothered to lift so much as a piece of posterboard to help her out, even though the person she's trying to help is someone whose misfortunes are all my fault in the first place. And my grade is starting to slide in Algebra again, and I don't even care.

Really, with all that weighing on my shoulders, what choice do I have but to turn on the Lifetime Movie Channel for Women? Maybe if I watch some movies about real-life women who've surmounted near impossible obstacles, I might find the courage to face my own.

Hey, it could happen.

Saturday. May 3. 7:30 p.m. half an hour before my party is to begin

I don't think turning on the Lifetime Movie Channel for Women was such a hot idea. All it did was make me feel inadequate. Really, I don't know who could watch movies like that and not feel bad about themselves. I mean, here is just a sample of what some of these women endured:

The Taking of Flight 847: The Uli Derickson Story

The Bionic Woman's Lindsay Wagner saves all but one of the passengers in this true story of a plane hijacking in the mid-eighties. In the movie, Uli convinces the hijackers to spare the lives of the passengers by singing a touching folk song, causing the hijackers' eyes to well up.

Unfortunately I don't know any folk songs, and the songs I do know — such as Bif Naked's 'I Love Myself Today (Uh-Huh)' — probably wouldn't soothe anyone, especially a hijacker.

The Abduction of Kari Swenson

Michael J. Fox's wife Tracey Pollan stars in the true story of an Olympic biathlete who gets kidnapped by hillbillies who want to make her their bride. Ew! As if camping isn't bad enough. Imagine having to camp with people who've never bathed. But Kari gets away and goes on to win the gold, and the bad guys go to jail, where they make them shave every day and brush their teeth.

However, I am no biathlete. I am not even an athlete. If I were kidnapped by hillbillies, I would probably just start crying until they let me go in disgust.

Cry for Help: the Tracey Thurman Story

Facts of Life's Jo get brutally assaulted by her husband while the cops are watching, then successfully sues the police for failing to protect her, striking a blow for victims of stalking everywhere.

But I have a bodyguard. If anybody tried to assault me, Lars would hit them with his stun gun.

Sudden Terror: The Hijacking of School Bus#17

Maria Conchita Alonso, fresh from her role as Amber in *The Running Man*, plays Marta Caldwell, the brave driver of a Special Ed. bus which is hijacked by a guy who is mad at the IRS. Her calm and gentle demeanour keeps the hijacker still long enough for a SWAT officer to shoot him in the head through the bus window, much to the horror of her Special Ed. charges, who are hit with the guy's blood spatter and brain tissue.

But I take a limo to school, so the chances of this happening to me are moot.

She Woke Up Pregnant

This is the true story of a woman whose dentist has sex with her while she is under anaesthesia for a root canal. Then the dentist has the nerve to say he and the patient had an affair and that she's making up the rape thing so her husband won't get mad about the new baby . . . until, that is, a female cop goes undercover as a patient and the cops use a lipstick camera to catch the dentist in the act of taking her shirt off!

But this would never happen to me as I have nothing in the chestal area that would be of interest even to a psychopathic dentist.

Miracle Landing

Connie Sellecca plays First Officer Mimi Thompkins, who manages successfully to land Flight 243 after its roof is ripped off mid-flight due to metal fatigue. She is not the only brave one on that flight, since there was also a flight attendant who kept checking on the people in the front of the plane where there was no roof, and telling them they were going to be fine even though they had giant pieces of aeroplane carpet stuck to their heads.

I would so never be able either to land a plane or tell people with massive head wounds that they were going to be fine, due to the fact that I would be barfing too hard.

Seriously, I don't know how anyone can be expected to just hop out of bed after viewing movies like that and feel all good about themselves.

Even worse, I happened to catch a few minutes of *Miracle Pets*, and I was forced to admit that, as a pet, Fat Louie is pretty much bottom of the barrel, intelligence-wise. I mean, on *Miracle Pets* they had a donkey that saved its owner from wild dogs; a parrot that saved its owners from a house fire; a dog that saved its owner from dying of insulin shock by gently shaking her until she ate some gumdrops, and a cat that noticed its owner was unconscious and sat on the auto-dial 911 button on the phone and miaowed until help arrived.

I am sorry, but Fat Louie would be no match for wild dogs, would probably hide in a fire, wouldn't know a gumdrop from a hole in the wall, and wouldn't know to sit on the 911 button if I were unconscious. In fact, if I were unconscious, Fat Louie would probably just sit by his food bowl and cry until Ronnie from next door finally went insane and got the superintendant to let her in to shut the cat up.

Even my cat is a failure.

Worse, Mom and Mr G had a fabulous time without me at B.J.'s. Well, except for the part where Mom totally had to pee but they were stuck in the middle of the Holland Tunnel, so she had to hold it until they came to the first Shell station on the other side, and when she ran to the ladies' room it turned out to be locked so she nearly ripped the arm off the gas station attendant grabbing the key from him.

But they found tons of Queen Amidala stuff on sale, including panties (for me, not the party guests, of course). My mom poked her head into my room when they got home to show me the Amidala panty six-pack she picked up, but I just couldn't work up any kind of enthusiasm about it, though I tried.

Maybe I have PMS.

Or maybe the weight of my new-found womanhood, seeing as how I'm fifteen now, is simply too much to bear.

And I really should be happy, because Mr G hung all these Queen Amidala streamers up all over the Loft, and strung flashing white Christmas lights all through the pipework on the ceiling and put a Queen Amidala mask on Mom's lifesize bust of Elvis. He even promised not to jam on his drums along with the music (a carefully selected mix put together by Michael, which includes all my favourite Destiny's Child

101

and Bree Sharp releases, even though Michael can't stand them).

WHAT IS WRONG WITH ME???? Is this all just because my boyfriend hasn't asked me to the prom yet? Why do I even care? Why can't I be happy with what I have? WHY CAN'T I JUST BE GLAD I EVEN HAVE A BOYFRIEND AND LEAVE IT AT THAT?

This party was such a bad idea. I am so not in a party mood. What was I even thinking, having a party? I AM AN UNPOPULAR NERD PRINCESS!!!!! UNPOPULAR NERD PRINCESSES SHOULD NOT HAVE PARTIES!!!!!!!!! NOT EVEN FOR THEIR UNPOPULAR NERD FRIENDS!!!!!!!!! No one is going to come. No one is going to come, and I'm going to end up sitting here all night with the twinkling Christmas lights and the stupid Queen Amidala streamers and the Cheetos and the Coke and Michael's mix, BY MYSELF.

Oh God, the buzzer just went off. Someone is here. Please God give me the strength to get through this night. Give me the strength of Uli, Kari, Tracey, Marta, that dental patient lady, Mimi and that flight attendant. Please, that's all I ask of you. Thanks.

Sunday, May 4, 2 a.m.

Well. That's it. It's over. My life is over.

I would like to thank all those who stood by me during the hard times — my mother, back before she became a one hundred and eighty pound quivering mass of bladderless hormones; Mr G, for attempting to salvage my GPA, and Fat Louie for just being, well, Fat Louie, even if he is totally useless when compared to the animals on *Miracle Pets*.

But nobody else. Because everybody else I know is obviously part of some nefarious plot to drive me to madness, just like Bertha Rochester in *Jane Eyre*.

Take Tina, for example. Tina, who shows up at my party and, first thing, grabs me by the arm and drags me into my room, where everybody is supposed to be leaving their coats, and tells me, 'Ling Su and I have got it all worked out. Ling Su'll keep your mom and Mr G busy, and then I will announce the game of Seven Minutes in Heaven. When it's your turn, get Michael in the closet and start kissing him and when you've reached the height of passion, ask him about the prom.'

'Tina!' I was really annoyed. And not just because I thought her plan was totally weak, either. No, I was miffed because Tina was wearing body glitter. Really! She had it

103

smeared all over her collarbones. How come I can't even seem to find body glitter in the store? And, if I did, would I have the coolness to smear it on my collarbones? No. Because I am too boring.

'We are not playing Seven Minutes in Heaven at my birthday party,' I informed her.

Tina looked crestfallen. 'Why not?'

'Because this is a nerd party! My God, Tina! We are nerds. We don't play Seven Minutes in Heaven. That is the kind of thing people like Lana and Josh play at their parties. At nerd parties, we play things like Spoon, or possibly Light as a Feather, Stiff as a Board. But not kissing games!'

But Tina was totally adamant that nerds DO play kissing games.

'Because if they don't,' she pointed out, 'then how do you think little nerds get made?'

I suggested that little nerds get made in the privacy of nerd homes after nerds marry, but Tina wasn't even listening any more. She flounced out into the main room to greet Boris, who'd actually, it turned out, arrived a half-hour before, but since he hadn't wanted to be the first one at the party had stood in my vestibule for thirty minutes, reading all the Chinese menus the delivery boys shove under the door.

'Where's Lilly?' I asked Boris, because I would have thought the two of them would arrive at the same time, seeing as how they are dating and all.

But Boris said he hadn't seen Lilly since the march on Les Hautes Manger that afternoon.

'She was at the front of the group,' he explained to me as he stood by the refreshment table (really our dining table) shoving Cheetos in his mouth. A surprising amount of orange powder got trapped between the spokes of his orthodontic brace. It was oddly fascinating to watch, in a completely gross way. 'You know, with her megaphone, leading the chants. That was the last I saw of her. I got hungry and stopped for a hot dog, and next thing I knew they had all marched on without me.'

I told Boris that that is, actually, the point of a march . . . that people are supposed to march, not wait for members of the group who'd stopped for hot dogs. Boris seemed kind of shocked to hear this, which I guess is not surprising, since he is from Russia, where marching of any kind was outlawed for many years, except marches for the glorification of Lenin, or whatever.

Anyway, Michael showed up next with the mix for the CD player. I'd thought about having his band play for my party, since they are always looking for gigs, but Mr G said no way, as he gets in enough trouble with our downstairs neighbour Verl just for playing his drums. A whole band might send Verl over the edge. Verl goes to bed promptly every night at 9 p.m. so he can be up before dawn to record the activity of our neighbours across the way, whom he believes are aliens sent to this planet to observe us and report back to the mother ship in preparation for eventual interplanetary warfare. The people across the way don't look like aliens to me, but they *are* German, so you can see why Verl might have made such a mistake.

Michael, as usual, looked incredibly hot. WHY does he always have to look so handsome, every time I see him? I mean, you would think I would get used to how he looks, seeing as how I see him practically every day . . . a couple of times a day, even.

But each and every time I see him, my heart gives this giant lurch. Like he's a present I'm just about to unwrap, or something. It's sick, this weakness I have for him. Sick, I tell you.

Anyway, Michael put the music on, and other people started to arrive, and everyone was milling around, talking about the march, and last night's *Farscape* marathon — everybody except for me, who hadn't taken part in either. Instead, I just ran around taking people's coats (because even though it was May it was still nippy out) and praying that everybody was having a good time and that no one would leave early or overhear my mother telling anyone who would listen about her Incredible Shrinking Bladder . . .

Then the doorbell rang and I went to answer it, and there was Lilly, standing with her arms round this dark-haired guy in a leather jacket.

'Hi!' Lilly said, looking all bubbly and excited. 'I don't think you two have met. Mia, this is Jangbu. Jangbu, this is Princess Amelia of Genovia. Or Mia, as we call her.'

I stared at Jangbu in shock. Not because, you know, Lilly had brought him to my party without asking first, or anything. But because, well, Lilly had her arm round his waist. She was practically hanging on him, for crying out loud. And her boyfriend, Boris, was right there, in the next room, trying to learn the electric slide from Shameeka . . .

'Mia,' Lilly said, stepping inside with a look of annoyance. 'Don't say hi, or anything.'

I said, 'Oh, sorry. Hi.'

Jangbu said hi back, and smiled. The truth was, Jangbu WAS incredibly good-looking, just like Lilly had said. In fact, he was way better looking than poor Boris. Well, I hate to admit it, but who isn't? Still, I never thought Lilly liked Boris for his looks, anyway. I mean, Boris is a musical genius and, as I happen to know, given the fact that I myself go out with one, they are not easy to find.

107

Fortunately Lilly had to let go of Jangbu long enough for him to take off his leather jacket when I offered to put it in the bedroom for him. So when Boris finally saw that she'd arrived and went over to say hello he didn't notice anything amiss. I took Jangbu and Lilly's jackets and wandered, in a daze, back towards my bedroom. I ran into Michael along the way, who grinned at me and said, 'Having fun yet?'

I just shook my head. 'Did you see that?' I asked him. 'Your sister and Jangbu?'

Michael looked towards them. 'No. What?'

'Nothing,' I said. I didn't want to cause Michael to blow up at Lilly the way Colin Hanks did when he caught his little sister, Kirsten Dunst, kissing his best friend in the movie *Get Over It*. Because even though I have never really noticed Michael harbouring protective feelings towards Lilly I am sure that is only because she has been dating Boris all this time, and Boris is one of Michael's friends and a mouth-breather, besides. I mean, you are not going to get too upset over your little sister going out with a mouth-breathing violinist. A hot, newly unemployed Sherpa, however . . . now that might be a different story.

And though you wouldn't know it to look at him Michael is very quick-tempered. I once saw him glare quite formidably at some construction workers who whistled at me and Lilly down on Sixth Ave. when we were coming out of Charlie Mom's. The last thing I needed at my party was for a fist fight to break out.

But Lilly managed to keep her hands off Jangbu for the next half-hour, during which I attempted to put aside my depression and join in on the fun, especially when everyone started jumping around, doing the Macarena, which Michael had jokingly put in the mix he'd made.

It's too bad there aren't more dances, other than the Time Warp and the Macarena, that everybody knows. You know how in movies like *She's All That* and *Footloose*, everybody starts doing the same dance at the same time? It would be so cool if that would happen sometime in like the cafeteria. Principal Gupta could be on the sound system, reading off the announcements, and suddenly somebody puts on the Yeah Yeah Yeahs or whatever and we all start dancing on the tables.

In olden times, everybody knew the same dances . . . like the minuet, and stuff. Too bad things can't be like olden times.

Except, of course, I wouldn't want to have wooden teeth or the pox.

Anyway, things were finally starting to look up, and I was actually having a pretty good time fooling around, when all of a sudden Tina was like, 'Mr G, we're out of Coke!' and

Mr G was like, 'How can that be? I bought seven flats of it at the drive-through liquor store this morning.'

But Tina insisted all the Coke was gone. I found out later she'd hidden it in the baby's room. But whatever. At the time, Mr G honestly thought there was no more Coke.

'Well, I'll run down to Grand Union and buy more,' he said, putting on his coat and going out.

That's when Ling Su asked my mom if she could see her slides. Ling Su, being an artist herself, knew exactly the right thing to say to my mother, a fellow artist, even if since she's been pregnant she's had to give up oils and work only in egg tempera.

No sooner had my mom whisked Ling Su into her bedroom to break out her slides than Tina turned off the music and announced that we would now be playing Seven Minutes in Heaven.

Everybody looked pretty excited about this — we certainly had never played Seven Minutes in Heaven at the last party we'd all been to, which had been at Shameeka's house. But Mr Taylor, Shameeka's dad, wasn't the type to fall for the 'Out of Coke' or 'Can I see your slides?' thing. He is way strict. He keeps the baseball bat he once hit a home run with in one corner of the room as a 'reminder' to the boys Shameeka dates of just what, exactly, he's capable of, should they get fresh with his daughter.

So the Seven Minutes in Heaven thing had everybody way stoked. Everybody, that is, except for Michael. Michael is not a big fan of Public Displays of Affection, and it turns out he is even less of a fan of being locked in a closet with his girlfriend. Not, he informed me, after Tina had gigglingly shut the closet door — closing the two of us in with Mom and Mr G's winter coats, the vacuum cleaner, the laundry cart and my wheelie suitcase — that he had anything against being in a dark enclosed space with me. It was the fact that, outside the door, everybody was listening that bugged him.

'Nobody's listening,' I told him. 'See? They turned the music back on.'

Which they had.

But I sort of had to agree with Michael. Seven Minutes in Heaven is a stupid game. I mean, it is one thing to make out with your boyfriend. It is quite another to do it in a closet, with everybody on the other side of the door knowing what you are doing. The ambiance is just not there.

It was dark in the closet — so dark I couldn't even see my own hand in front of my face, let alone Michael. Plus, it smelt funny. This, I knew, was on account of the vacuum cleaner. It had been a while since anybody — namely, me, since my mom never remembers, and Mr G doesn't understand our vacuum cleaner, on account of it being so old — had emptied the vacuum bag, and it was filled to the brim with orange cat fur and the pieces of kitty litter Fat Louie is always tracking across the floor. Since it was scented kitty litter, it smelt a little like pine. But not necessarily in a good way.

'So we really have to stay in here for seven minutes?' Michael wanted to know.

'I guess,' I said.

'What if Mr G gets back and finds us in here?'

'He'll probably kill you,' I said.

'Well,' Michael said. 'Then I'd better give you something to remember me by.'

Then he took me in his arms and started kissing me.

I have to admit, after that, I kind of started thinking Seven Minutes in Heaven wasn't such a bad game after all. In fact, I sort of began to like it. It was nice to be there in the dark, with Michael's body all pressed up to mine, and his tongue in my mouth, and all. I guess because I couldn't see anything, my sense of smell was that much stronger, or something, because I could smell Michael's neck really well. It smelt super nice — way better than the vacuum-cleaner bag. The smell sort of made me want to jump on him. I can't really explain it any other way. But I honestly wanted to jump on Michael.

Instead of jumping on him, which I didn't think he'd

enjoy — nor would it be socially acceptable . . . plus, you know, all the coats were sort of impeding our ability to move around a lot — I tore my lips from his, and said, not even thinking about Tina, or Uli Derickson, or even what I was doing, but sort of lost in the heat of the moment, 'So, Michael, what is up with the prom? Are we going, or not?'

To which Michael replied, with a chuckle, as his lips nuzzled my own neck (though I highly doubt he was smelling it), 'The prom? Are you crazy? The prom's even stupider than this game.'

At which point, I sort of broke our embrace and took a step backwards, right on to Mr G's hockey stick. Only I didn't care, because, you know, I was so shocked.

'What do you mean?' I demanded. If it hadn't been so dark, I so would have run my searching gaze across Michael's face, looking for some sign he was joking. As it was, however, I just had to listen really hard.

'Mia,' Michael said, reaching for me. For somebody who thought Seven Minutes in Heaven was such a stupid game, he seemed to be kind of into it. 'You've got to be kidding. I'm not exactly the prom type.'

But I slapped his hands away. It was hard, you know, to see them in the dark, but it wasn't like there was much chance of missing. The only other thing in front of me, besides Michael, was coats.

'What do you mean, you're not the prom type?' I wanted to know. 'You're a Senior. You're graduating. You have to go to the prom. Everybody does it.'

'Yeah,' Michael said. 'Well, everybody does lots of lame stuff. But that doesn't mean I'm going to too. I mean, come on, Mia. Proms are for the Josh Richters of the world.'

'Oh, really?' I said, sounding very cold, even to my own ears. But that was probably on account of how super attuned they were to everything, seeing as how I couldn't see. My ears, I mean. 'What, then, do the Michael Moscovitzes of the world do on prom night?'

'I don't know,' Michael said. 'We could do more of *this*, if you want.'

By *this*, of course, he meant making out in a closet. I did not even credit that with a response.

'Michael,' I said, in my most princessy voice. 'I'm serious. If you don't plan on going to the prom, just what, exactly, do you intend to do instead?'

'I don't know,' Michael said, sounding genuinely baffled by my question. 'Go bowling?'

BOWLING!!!!!!!!!!!!!!!! MY BOYFRIEND WOULD RATHER GO BOWLING ON HIS PROM NIGHT THAN GO TO THE PROM!!!!!!!!!!!!!!

Does he not have an ounce of romantic feeling in

114

his body? He must, because he got me that snowflake necklace . . . the necklace that I haven't taken off, not even once, since he gave it to me. How can the man who gave me that necklace be the same man who would rather go *bowling* on his prom night than go to the prom?

He must have sensed that I was not taking kindly to this news, since he went, 'Mia, come on. Admit it. The prom is the corniest thing in the world. I mean, you spend a ton of money on some rented penguin suit you can't even get comfortable in, then spend a ton more money on dinner somewhere fancy that probably isn't half as good as Number One Noodle Son, then you go and stand around in some gymnasium——'

'Maxim's,' I corrected him. 'Your Senior Prom is taking place at Maxim's.'

'Whatever,' Michael said. 'So you go and eat stale cookies and dance to really, really bad music with a bunch of people you can't stand and who you never want to see again——'

'Like me, you mean?' I was practically crying, I was so hurt. 'You never want to see me again? Is that it? You're just going to graduate and go off to college and forget all about me?'

'Mia,' Michael said, in quite a different tone of voice. 'Of course not. I wasn't talking about you. I was talking about people like . . . well, like Josh and those guys. You know that. What's the matter with you?'

But I couldn't tell Michael what was the matter with me. Because what was the matter with me was that my eyes had filled up with tears and my throat had closed up and I'm not sure but I think my nose had started to run. Because all of a sudden I realized that my boyfriend had no intention of asking me to the prom. Not because he was going to ask someone more popular instead, or anything. Like Andrew McCarthy in *Pretty in Pink*. But because my boyfriend, Michael Moscovitz, the person I loved most in the whole world (with the exception of my cat), the man to whom I had pledged my heart for all eternity, had absolutely no interest at all in attending HIS OWN SENIOR PROM!!!

I really can't say what would have happened next if Boris hadn't suddenly ripped the closet door open and yelled, 'Time's up!' Maybe Michael would have heard me sniffling and realized I was crying and asked me why. And then, after he'd drawn me tenderly into his arms, I might have told him in a broken voice, while resting my head against his manly chest.

And then he might have sweetly kissed the top of my head and murmured, 'Oh, my darling, I didn't know,' and sworn then and there that he would do anything, anything in the world, to see my doe eyes shine again, and that if I wanted to go to the prom, well then, by God, we'd go to the prom.

Only that's so not what happened. What happened instead was that Michael blinked at all the sudden light, and held up an arm to shield his eyes, and so never even saw that my own eyes were tear-filled and that my nose might possibly have been running . . . although this would have been horribly unprincesslike and probably didn't even happen.

Besides, I nearly forgot my grief, I was so astounded by what happened next. And that was that Lilly went, 'My turn! My turn!'

And everyone got out of her way as she went barrelling towards the closet . . .

Only the hand she reached for — the man whom she chose to accompany her for her Seven Minutes in Heaven — was not the pale, soft hand of the violin virtuoso with whom, for the past eight months, Lilly had been sharing furtive French kisses and Sunday morning dim sum. The hand Lilly reached for was not one belonging to Boris Pelkowski, mouth-breather and sweater tucker-inner. No, the hand Lilly reached for belonged to none other than Jangbu Pinasa, the hot Sherpa busboy.

Stunned silence roared through the room — well, except

for the wailing of the Sahara Hotnights on the stereo — as Lilly thrust a startled Jangbu into my hall coat closet, then quickly went in after him. We all stood there, blinking at the closed door, not knowing quite what to do.

At least, *I* didn't know what to do. I looked over at Tina, and I could tell by the shocked expression on her face that *she* didn't know what to do, either.

Michael, on the other hand, seemed to know what to do. He laid a sympathetic hand on Boris's shoulder and said, 'Tough break, man,' then went and grabbed a handful of Cheetos.

TOUGH BREAK, MAN?????? That is what boys say to one another when they see that their friend's heart has just been ripped from his chest and tossed upon the floor?

I couldn't believe Michael could be so cavalier. I mean, what about the whole Colin Hanks thing? Why wasn't he tearing that closet door open, hauling Jangbu Pinasa out of it, and beating him to a bloody pulp? I mean, Lilly was his little sister, for God's sake. Didn't he have an ounce of protective feeling towards her?

Completely forgetting about my despair over the whole prom thing — I think the shock of seeing Lilly's eagerness to lock lips with someone other than her boyfriend had numbed my senses — I followed Michael to the refreshment table and said, 'That's it? That's all you're going to do?'

He looked at me questioningly. 'About what?'

'About your sister!' I cried. 'And Jangbu!'

'What do you want me to do about it?' Michael asked. 'Haul him out and hit him?'

'Well,' I said. 'Yes!'

'Why?' Michael drank some 7-Up, since there wasn't any Coke. 'I don't care who my sister locks herself into the closet with. If it were you, then I'd hit the guy. But it's not you, it's Lilly. Lilly, as I believe she's amply proved over the years, can take care of herself.' He held a bowl out towards me. 'Cheeto?'

Cheetos! Who could think of food at a time like this?

'No, thank you,' I said. 'But aren't you at all worried that Lilly's—' I broke off, uncertain how to continue. Michael helped me out.

'Been swept off her feet by the guy's rugged Sherpa good looks?' Michael shook his head. 'Looked to me like if anybody is being taken advantage of, it's Jangbu. The poor guy doesn't seem to know what hit him.'

'B-but . . . ' I stammered. 'But what about Boris?'

Michael looked over at Boris, who had slumped down on to the futon couch, his head cradled in his hands. Tina had rushed over to him and was trying to offer sisterly balm to his wounded feelings by telling him that Lilly was probably only showing Jangbu what the inside of a real American coat closet looked like. Even I didn't think she sounded very convincing, and I am very easily convinced by almost anything. For instance, in convocations where we are forced to listen to the debate team, I almost always agree with whichever team is talking at the moment, no matter what they're saying.

'Boris'll get over it,' Michael said, and reached for the chips and dip.

I don't understand boys. I really don't. I mean, if it had been MY little sister in the closet with Jangbu, I would have been furious with rage. And if it had been MY Senior Prom I'd have been falling all over myself in an effort to secure tickets before they were all gone.

But that's me, I guess.

Anyway, before any of us had a chance to do anything more, the front door to the Loft opened and Mr G came in, carrying bags of more Coke.

'I'm home,' Mr G called, putting the bags down and starting to take off his windbreaker. 'I picked up some ice too. I figured we might be running out by now . . . '

Mr G's voice trailed off. That's because he'd opened the hall closet door to put away his coat and found Lilly and Jangbu in there, making out.

Well, that was the end of my party. Mr Gianini is no Mr Taylor, but he's still pretty strict. Also, being a high-school teacher and all, he is not unfamiliar with games like Seven Minutes in Heaven. Lilly's excuse — that she and Jangbu had gotten locked into the closet together accidentally — didn't exactly fly with him. Mr G said he thought it was time for everybody to go home. Then he got Hans, my limo driver, who we'd arranged beforehand to take everybody home after the party, to make sure that when he dropped off Lilly and Michael, Jangbu didn't go inside with them, and that Lilly went all the way into her building, up the elevator and everything, so she didn't try to sneak down and meet Jangbu later, like at Blimpie's or whatever.

And now I am lying here, a broken shell of a girl . . . fifteen years old, and yet so much older in so many ways. Because I know now what it is like to see all of your hopes and dreams crushed beneath the soulless heel of despair. I saw it in Boris's eyes, as he watched Lilly and Jangbu emerge from that closet, looking flushed and sweaty, Lilly actually *tugging on the bottom of her shirt* (I cannot believe Lilly got to second base before I did. And with a guy she'd known for a mere twenty-four hours, as well — not to mention the fact that she did it in MY hallway closet).

But Boris's eyes weren't the only ones registering despair tonight. My own have a distinctly hollow look to them. I noticed tonight as I was brushing my teeth before bed. It is no mystery why, of course. My eyes have a haunted look to them because I am haunted . . . haunted by the spectre of the dream of a prom that I know now will never be. Never will I, dressed in off-one-shoulder black, rest my head upon the shoulder of Michael (in a tux) at his Senior Prom. Never will I enjoy the stale cookies he mentioned, nor the look on Lana Weinberger's face when she sees that she is not the only freshman girl besides Shameeka in attendance.

My prom dream is over. And so, I am afraid, is my life.

Sunday, May 4, 9 a.m., the Loft

It is very hard to be sunk in the black well of despair when your mother and stepfather get up at the crack of dawn and put on The Donnas while making their breakfast waffles. Why can't they go quietly to church to hear the word of the Lord, like normal parents, and leave me to wallow in my own grief? I swear it is enough to make me contemplate moving to Genovia.

Except, of course, there I would be expected to get up and go to church as well. I guess I should be thanking my lucky stars that my mother and her husband are godless heathens. But they could at least turn it DOWN.

Sunday, May 4, noon, the Loft

My plan for the day was to stay in bed with the covers up over my head until it was time to go to school on Monday morning. That is what people who have had their reason for living cruelly snatched from them do: stay in bed as much as possible.

This plan was unfairly destroyed, however, by my mother, who just came barrelling in (at her current size, she can't help but barrel everywhere she goes) and sat down on the edge of the bed, nearly crushing Fat Louie, who had slunk down underneath the covers with me and was snoozing at my toes. After screaming because Fat Louie had sunk all his claws into her rear end, right through my duvet, my mom apologized for barging in on my grief-stricken solitude, but — she said — she thought it was time we had A Little Talk.

It is never a good thing when my mom thinks it is a time for A Little Talk. The last time she and I had A Little Talk, I was forced to listen to a very long speech about body image and my supposedly distorted one. My mother was very worried that I was contemplating using my Christmas money for breast-enhancement surgery, and she wanted me to know what a bad idea she thought this was, because women's obsession with their looks has got completely out of control. In Korea, for instance, thirty per cent of women in their twenties have had some form of plastic surgery, ranging from cheekbone and jawbone shaving to eye slicing and calf-muscle removal (for slimmer calves) in order to achieve a more Western look. This as opposed to three per cent of women in the US who have had plastic surgery for purely aesthetic purposes.

The good news? America is NOT the most image-obsessed country in the world. The bad news? Too many women outside our culture feel pressured to change their looks to better emulate ours, thinking Western standards of beauty are more important than their own country's, because that is what they see on old reruns of shows like *Baywatch* and *Friends*. Which is wrong, just wrong, because Nigerian women are just as beautiful as women from LA or Manhattan. Just in a different way.

As awkward as THAT chat had been (I was not contemplating using my Christmas money for breast-enhancement surgery: I was contemplating using my Christmas money for a complete set of Shania Twain CDs, but of course I couldn't ADMIT that to anyone, so my mom naturally thought it was something to do with my boobs), the one we had today really takes the cake as far as mother/daughter talks go.

Because of course today was THE mother/daughter talk. Not the 'Honey, your body is changing and soon you'll have a different use for those sanitary napkins of mine you stole to make into beds for your Star Wars action figures' talk. Oh no. Today was the 'You're fifteen now and you have a boyfriend and last night my husband caught you and your little friends playing Seven Minutes in Heaven and so I think it's time we discussed You Know What' talk.

I have recorded our conversation here as best I could so that when I have my own daughter I can make sure NEVER, EVER to say any of these things to her, remembering how INCREDIBLY AND UTTERLY STUPID THEY MADE ME FEEL WHEN MY OWN MOTHER SAID THEM TO ME. As far as I'm concerned, my own daughter can learn about sex from the Lifetime Movie Channel for Women, like everybody else on the planet.

Mom: Mia, I just heard from Frank that Lilly and her new friend Jambo—

Me: Jangbu.

Mom: Whatever. That Lilly and her new friend were, er, kissing in our hall closet. Apparently, you were all playing some sort of make-out game, Five Minutes in the Closet—

Me: Seven Minutes in Heaven.

Mom: Whatever. The point is, Mia, you're fifteen now. You're pretty much an adult, and I know that you and Michael are very much a couple. It's only natural that you'd be curious about sex . . . perhaps even experimenting—

Me: MOM!!!! GROSS!!!!!!!!!

Mom: There's nothing gross about sexual relations between two people who love one another, Mia. Of course I would prefer it if you waited until you were older. Until you were in college, maybe. Or your mid-thirties, anyway. However, I know only too well what it is like to be a slave to your hormones, so it's important that you take the appropriate precau—

Me: I mean, it's gross to talk about it with my MOTHER.

Mom: Well, yes, I know. Or rather, I don't know, since my own mother would have sooner dropped dead than have mentioned any of this to me. However, I think it is important for mothers and daughters to be open with one another about these things. For instance, Mia, if you ever feel that you need to talk about birth control, I can make you an appointment with my gynaecologist, Dr Brandeis—

Me: MOM!!!!!!!!!!!!!! MICHAEL AND I ARE NOT HAVING SEX!!!!!!!!!!!!!!!!!

Mom: Well, I'm glad to hear that, honey, since you are a bit young. But if the two of you should decide to, I want to make sure you have all your facts straight. For instance, are you and your friends aware that diseases like AIDS can be transmitted through oral sex as well as—

Me: YES, MOM, I KNOW THIS. I AM TAKING HEALTH AND SAFETY THIS SEMESTER, REMEMBER?????

Mom: Mia, sex is nothing to be embarrassed about. It is one of the basic human needs, such as water, food and social interaction. It is important that if you choose to become sexually active, you protect yourself.

Oh, you mean like *you* did, Mom, when you got knocked up by Mr Gianini? Or by DAD?????

Only of course I didn't say this. Because, you know, what would be the point? Instead I just nodded and went, 'OK, Mom. Thanks, Mom. I'll be sure to, Mom,' hoping she'd finally give up and go away.

Only it didn't work. She just kept hanging around, like one of Tina's little sisters whenever I'm over at the Hakim Babas' and Tina and I want to sneak a look at her dad's *Playboy* collection. Really, you can learn a lot from the *Playboy* adviser, from what kind of car stereo works best in a Porsche Boxter to how to tell if your husband is having an affair with his personal assistant. Tina says it is a good idea to know your enemy, which is why she reads her dad's copies of *Playboy* whenever she gets the chance . . . though we both agree that, judging from the stuff in this magazine, the enemy is very, very weird.

And oddly fixated with cars.

Finally my mom ran out of steam. The Little Talk just kind of petered out. She sat there for a minute, looking around at my room, which is only minorly a disaster area. I am pretty neat, overall, because I always feel like I have to clean my room before I can start on my homework. Something about a clear environment making for clear thinking. I don't know. Maybe it's just because homework is so boring I'll take any excuse to put off doing it.

'Mia,' my mom said after a long pause. 'Why are you still in bed at noon on a Sunday? Isn't this when you usually meet your friends for dim sum?'

I shrugged. I didn't want to admit to my mom that dim sum was probably the last thing on anybody's mind this morning . . . I mean, seeing as how apparently Lilly and Boris were broken up now.

'I hope you aren't upset with Frank,' my mom went on, 'for ruining your party. But really, Mia, you and Lilly are old enough to know better than to play silly games like Seven

Minutes in Heaven. What on earth is wrong with playing Spoon?'

I shrugged some more. What was I going to say? That the reason I was so upset had nothing to do with Mr G, and everything to do with the fact that my boyfriend didn't want to go to the prom? Lilly was right: the prom is just a stupid pagan dance ritual. Why did I even care?

'Well,' my mom said, climbing awkwardly to her feet. 'If you want to stay in bed all day, I'm certainly not going to stop you. There's no place else I'd rather be, I'll admit. But then, I'm an old pregnant lady, not a fifteen-year-old.'

Then she left. THANK GOD. I can't believe she tried to have a sex talk with me. About *Michael*. I mean, doesn't she know Michael and I haven't gotten past first base? No one I know has, with the exception, of course, of Lana. At least I assume Lana has, judging by what got spray-painted about her across the gymnasium wall over Spring Break. And now Lilly, of course.

God. My best friend has been to more bases than I have. And *I* am the one who is supposed to have found my soulmate. Not *her*.

Life is so unfair.

Sunday, May 4, 7 p.m., the Loft

I guess it must be Check on Mia's Mental Health Day, since everybody is calling to find out how I am. That was my dad on the phone just now. He wanted to know how my party went. While on the one hand this is a good thing — it means neither Mom nor Mr G mentioned the whole Seven Minutes in Heaven thing to him, which wouldn't have made him too ballistic or anything — it was also kind of a bad thing, since it meant I had to lie to him. While lying to my dad is easier than lying to my mom, because my dad, never having been a young girl, doesn't know the kind of capacity young girls have to tell terrific whoppers — and apparently isn't aware that my nostrils flare when I lie, either — it is still sort of nerve-racking. I mean, he IS a cancer survivor, after all. It seems sort of mean to lie to someone who is, basically, like Lance Armstrong. Except without all the Tour de France wins.

But whatever. I told him the party went great, blah blah blah.

Good thing he wasn't in the same room with me. He'd have noticed my nostrils flaring like crazy.

No sooner had I hung up the phone with my dad than it rang again, and I snatched it up, thinking it might be, oh,

I don't know, MY BOYFRIEND. You would have thought Michael might have called me at some point during the day, just to see how I was. You know, whether or not I was crippled with grief over the whole prom thing.

But apparently Michael is not all that concerned for my mental health, because not only has he not called, but the person on the other end of the phone when I eagerly snatched it up was about as far from being Michael as you can get.

It was, in fact, Grandmère.

Our conversation went like this:

Grandmère: Amelia, it is your grandmother. I need you to reserve the night of Wednesday the seventh. I've been asked to dine at Le Cirque with my old friend the Sultan of Brunei, and I want you to accompany me. And I don't want to hear any nonsense about how the Sultan needs to give up his Rolls because it is contributing to the destruction of the ozone layer. You need more culture in your life, and that's final. I'm tired of hearing about *Miraculous Pets* and the Lifetime Channel for Stay at Home Mothers or whatever it is you're always watching on the television. It's time you met some interesting people, and not the ones you see on TV, or those so-called artists your mother is always having over for girls' Bingo night, or whatever it is.

Me: OK, Grandmère. Whatever you say, Grandmère.

What, I ask you, is wrong with that answer? Really? What part of *OK, Grandmère. Whatever you say, Grandmère* would any NORMAL grandmother find suspicious? Of course, I'm forgetting my grandmother is far from normal. Because she was all over me, right away.

Grandmère: Amelia. What is wrong with you? Out with it, I haven't much time. I'm supposed to be dining with the Duc di Bormazo.

Me: Nothing's wrong, Grandmère. I'm just . . . I'm a little depressed, that's all. I didn't get such a good grade on my last Algebra quiz, and I'm a little down about it . . .

Grandmère: *Pfuit*. What is it REALLY, Mia? And make it snappy.

Me: Oh, all RIGHT. It's Michael. Remember that prom thing I told you about? Well, he doesn't want to go.

Grandmère: I knew it. He's still in love with that housefly girl, isn't he? He's taking her, is he? Well, never mind. I have Prince Harry's mobile phone number here some place. I'll give him a ring, and he can take his private jet over and take you to the little dance, if you want. That will show that unappreciative—

133

Me: No, Grandmère. Michael doesn't want to take someone else. He doesn't want to go at all. He . . . he thinks the prom is lame.

Grandmère: Oh . . . for . . . the . . . love . . . of . . . heaven. Not one of those.

Me: Yes, Grandmère. I'm afraid so.

Grandmère: Well, never mind. Your grandfather was the same way. Do you know that if I had left it up to him we'd have been married in a clerk's office, and gone to a *coffee shop* for lunch afterwards? The man simply had no understanding of romance, let alone the public's need for PAGEANTRY.

Me: Yes. Well. That's why I'm a little down today. Now, if you don't mind, Grandmère, I really have to start on my homework. I have a story due to the paper in the morning too . . .

I didn't mention that it was a story about HER. Well, more or less. It was the story about the incident at Les Hautes Manger. According to the *Sunday Times*, the restaurant's management was still refusing to take Jangbu back on. So Lilly's march had been for nothing. Well, except that it had apparently gotten her a new boyfriend.

Grandmère: Yes, yes, get to work. You have to keep your grades up, or your father will give me another one of his lectures about forcing you to concentrate too much on royal matters and not enough on trigonometry or whatever it is you seem to be having so much trouble with. And don't worry too much about the situation with *that boy*. He'll come round, same as your grandfather did. You just have to find the right incentive. Goodbye.

Incentive? What was Grandmère talking about? What kind of incentive would make Michael come round to the idea of going to the prom? I couldn't think of a single thing that might make him get over this obviously deeply rooted prejudice he had against it.

Except possibly if the prom were a combo prom/*Star Wars*/*Star Trek*/*Lord of the Rings*/computer convention.

Sunday, May 4, 9 p.m., the Loft

I know why Michael never called. Because he emailed me instead. I just didn't check my messages until I turned on my computer to type up my story for the *Atom*.

LinuxRulz: Mia – Hope you didn't get in too much trouble over the closet thing from last night. Mr G is a cool guy, though. I can't imagine he was too upset, after his initial blow-up.

Things have been pretty tense here, what with the whole Lilly/Boris break up. I am trying to stay out of it, and I strongly recommend, for your sanity's sake, you do the same. It's their problem, NOT OURS. I know how you are, Mia, and I really mean it when I say you're better off staying out of it. It's not worth it.

I'll be around all day if you want to give me a call. If you aren't grounded or whatever, maybe we can get together for dim sum? Or if you want I can come over later to help with your Algebra homework. Just let me know.

Love – Michael

Well. Judging from the tone of THAT, I guess Michael isn't feeling too bad about the whole prom thing. It's almost as if he doesn't KNOW he's ripped out my heart and torn it into little pieces.

Which, considering the fact that I didn't exactly tell him how I felt, might actually be true. That he doesn't know, I mean.

But ignorance, as Grandmère is fond of saying, is no excuse.

I would also hazard a guess from the unconcerned tone of that email that the Drs Moscovitz have not been paying visits to Michael's room, telling HIM about birth control and the richness of the human sexual experience. Oh no. That kind of thing always ends up being the girl's problem. Even if your boyfriend, like mine, is a staunch supporter of women's rights.

Well, at least he wrote. That's more than can be said for my so-called best friend. You would think that Lilly might at least have called to apologize for ruining my party. (Well, really it was Tina who ruined it, with her stupid Seven Minutes in Heaven idea. But Lilly is the one who killed it spiritually by making out with a guy who is not her boyfriend in front of said boyfriend. Well, practically.)

But I have heard nary a word from that ungrateful Boris-dumper. Far be it for me to cast stones at anyone for dating one guy while liking another . . . I mean, didn't I do that just last semester? Still, I didn't MAKE OUT with Michael before formally parting ways with Kenny. I had THAT much integrity, anyway.

And of course, I can't really blame Lilly for liking Jangbu more than Boris. I mean, come on. The guy is hot. And Boris is so . . . not.

Still. It wasn't very nice of her. I'm dying to know what she has to say for herself.

So is everybody else, apparently. Since I logged on, I've been bombarded with instant messages — from everybody but the guilty party concerned.

From Tina:

Iluvromance: Mia, are you all right? I was SO EMBARRASSED for you last night when Mr G caught Lilly and Jangbu in the closet. Was he REALLY mad? I mean, I know he was mad, but was he HOMICIDAL? God, I hope you're not dead. Like that he didn't kill you. That would SUCK if you got grounded, with the prom next week.

What did he say, anyway? Michael, I mean? When the two of you were in the closet together?

By the way, have you heard from Lilly? That was SO WEIRD last night. I mean, with her and Jangbu,

138

right in front of poor Boris. I felt so SORRY for him. He was practically crying – did you notice? And what was with her shirt? When she came out of the closet, I mean. Did you see that? Write back. T.

From Shameeka:

Beyonce Is Me: Oh my God, Mia, that party last night was da BOMB!!!!!!!!! If only Jeff and I had got a turn in that closet, I might finally have got a little action in my Victoria's Secrets, if you know what I mean. Just kidding. LOL. Anyway, could you believe that Lilly/Jangbu thing? What was THAT about? Is Mr G going to tell her DAD? Oh my God, if my dad found out I'd gone into the closet with a guy who'd already graduated from HS, I would be SO DEAD. Actually I'd be dead if I went into the closet with any guy . . . Anyway, have you heard from her? W/B with the DIRT!!!!!!!!!!!!!!

~Shameeka~

PS Did you talk to Michael about the prom? WHAT DID HE SAY????????????????????????

From Ling Su:

painturgurl: Mia, your mom is SUCH a good artist —
her slides were INCREDIBLE. By the way, what
HAPPENED while I was in her bedroom? Shameeka
said Mr G caught Lilly and that busboy guy in the
closet together? But surely she must have meant
Lilly and Boris? What was Lilly doing in the closet
with somebody other than Boris? Are they broken
up, or something? — Ling Su

PS Do you think your mom would let me borrow
her sable brushes? Just to try? I never used a really
nice brush before and I want to see if it makes any
difference before I go down to Pearl Paint and
spend a year's allowance on them.

PPS Did Michael ask you to the prom yet??????????

But those were nothing compared to the email I got from
Boris:

JoshBell2: Mia, I was wondering if you had heard
anything today from Lilly. I have been calling her
house all day, but Michael says she's not there. She

isn't with you, is she (I hope)? I am really afraid I might have done something to upset her. Why else would she have picked that other guy to go into the closet with last night? Did she mention anything to you, you know, about being upset with me? I know I stopped for that hot dog during her march, but I was really hungry. She knows I am slightly hypoglycaemic and need to eat every hour and a half.

Please, if you hear from her, let me know? I don't care if it turns out she's mad at me. I just want to know if she's all right. – Boris Pelkowski

I could kill Lilly for this. I really could. This is worse than that time she ran off with my cousin Hank. Because at least then there was no closet business.

God! It's so hard when your best friend is a genius riot-girl feminist/socialist champion of the common man.

It really is.

Monday, May 5, Homeroom

Well, I found out where Lilly was all day yesterday. Mr G showed me at the breakfast table. It was on the front page of the *New York Times*. Here is the article. I cut it out to save for posterity's sake. Also as a model for how my next article for the *Atom* should go, since I know Lesley is going to make me cover this story as well:

CITY-WIDE BUSBOY STRIKE

Manhattan – Restaurant workers city wide have thrown down their dish towels in an effort to show solidarity with Jangbu Pinasa, a fellow busboy who was dismissed from the four-star uptown brasserie, Les Hautes Manger, last Thursday night after a run-in involving the Dowager Princess of Genovia.

Witnesses say Pinasa, 18, was passing through the restaurant bearing a tray laden with dishware when he tripped and inadvertently spilt soup on the Dowager Princess. Pierre Jupe, manager of Les Hautes Manger, says Pinasa had already received a verbal warning due to another tray he'd dropped earlier in the evening. 'The guy is a klutz, plain and simple,' Jupe, 42, told reporters.

Pinasa's supporters, however, tell a different story. There is reason to believe the busboy did not simply lose his balance, but tripped over a customer's dog. New York City Health Department regulations require that only service animals, such as Seeing Eye dogs, be allowed inside establishments in which food is served to the public. If Les Hautes Manger is proven to have allowed customers to bring their dogs into the dining area, the restaurant could be subject to fines and even shut down.

'There was no dog,' restaurant owner Jean St Luc told reporters. 'The rumour about a dog is nothing but that, a rumour. Our customers would never bring a dog into our dining room. They are too well bred.'

Rumours of a dog – or a large rat – persist, however. Several witnesses claim they spotted an apparently hairless creature, approximately the size of a cat or large rat, darting in and out of the dining tables. A few mentioned that they thought the animal was some sort of pet of the Dowager Princess's, who was at the restaurant to celebrate the fifteenth birthday of her granddaughter, New York City's own royal, Princess of Genovia, Mia Thermopolis Renaldo.

Whatever the reason behind Pinasa's dismissal, busboys throughout the city have vowed to continue their work-stoppage until his job is restored. While restaurateurs insist that their dining establishments will remain open, busboys or not, there is reason for concern. Most waiters and waitresses, used only to taking orders and serving food, not clearing the used plates, may find themselves overburdened. Already some are discussing a sympathy strike to support the busboys, many of whom are illegal immigrants who work off the books, generally for less than the minimum wage and without such benefits as vacation or sick days, health insurance or retirement plans.

Regardless, city restaurants will struggle to remain open – though strike sponsors would like nothing better than to see the Metro area's dining community suffer for what they see as decades of neglect and condescension.

'Busboys have long been the butt of everyone's jokes,' says strike supporter Lilly Moscovitz, 15, who helped organize an impromptu march on City Hall on Sunday. 'It's time the Mayor and everyone else in this city woke up and smelt the dirty dishwater: without busboys, this city's name is mud.'

I seriously can't believe this. This whole thing has got way out of control. And all because of Rommel!!!! Well, and Lilly.

I truly couldn't believe it when Hans pulled up in

front of the Moscovitzes' building this morning, and Lilly was standing there next to Michael, looking as if butter wouldn't melt in her mouth. I actually don't know what that expression means, but Mamaw says it all the time, so it must mean something bad. And it does kind of fit how Lilly looked. Like she was just SOOOOOOOOO pleased with herself.

I glared at her and went, 'Talked to Boris yet, Lilly?' I didn't even say anything to Michael, on account of still being kind of mad at him over the whole prom thing. It was really hard to be mad at him because, of course, it was morning and he looked really, really good, all freshly shaved and smooth-faced, and like his neck would smell better than ever. And, of course, he is the best boyfriend of all time, since he wrote me that song and gave me the snowflake necklace and all of that.

But whatever. I have to be mad at him. Because that is the most absurd thing I've heard of, a guy not wanting to go to his own senior prom. I could understand if he didn't have a date or whatever, but Michael so totally DOES have a date. ME!!!!!!!!!!! And doesn't he know that by not taking me to his senior prom he is totally depriving me of the one memory of high school that I might actually be able to recall without shuddering? A memory I might be able to cherish, and even show my grandchildren photos of?

No, of course Michael doesn't know this, because I haven't told him. But how can I? I mean, he should know. If he is my true soulmate, he should KNOW without my having to tell him. It is perfectly common knowledge throughout our set that I have seen the movie *Pretty in Pink* forty-seven times. Does he think I watched it all those times because of my fondness for the actor who played the Duck Man?

But Lilly totally blew off my Boris question.

'You should have been there yesterday, Mia,' she said. 'On the march on City Hall, I mean. We had to have been a thousand people strong. It was totally empowering. It brought tears to my eyes, seeing the people come together like that to help further the cause of the working man.'

'You know what else brought tears to someone's eyes?' I asked her pointedly. 'You making out in the closet with Jangbu. That brought tears to your boyfriend's eyes. You remember your boyfriend, BORIS, don't you, Lilly?'

But Lilly just looked out the window at all the flowers that had sprung as if by magic from the dirt in the median on Park Avenue (actually, there's nothing magic about it: NYC parks employees plant them fully grown in the dead of night). 'Oh, look,' she said innocently. 'Spring has sprung.'

Talk about cold. I swear, sometimes I don't even know why I am friends with her.

Monday, May 5. Bio.

So . . .

> So what?

So did he ask you last night?????

> Didn't you hear?

Hear what?

> Michael doesn't believe in the prom. He thinks it's
> lame.

NO!!!!!!!!!!!!!!!!!!!!!

> Yes. Oh, Shameeka, what am I going to do? I've
> been dreaming of going to the prom with Michael
> my whole life, practically. Well, at least since
> we started dating, anyway. I want everyone to
> look at us dancing and know once and for all
> that I am the property of Michael Moscovitz.
> Even though I know that's sexist and no one can
> ever be the property of another human being.
> Except . . . except I so want to be Michael's
> property!!!!!!!!!!!!!!!!

I hear you. So what are you going to do?

What CAN I do? Nothing.

Um . . . you could try talking to him about it.

ARE YOU CRAZY????? Michael said he thinks the prom is LAME. If I tell him it's always been my secret fantasy to go to the prom with the man I love, what does that make me? Hello. That would make *me* lame.

Michael would never think you're lame, Mia. He loves you. I mean, maybe if he knew how you really felt, he'd come around to the whole prom thing.

Shameeka, I'm sorry, but I really think you've seen too many episodes of *Seventh Heaven*.

It's not my fault. It's the only show my dad'll let me watch.

Monday, May 5, Gifted and Talented

I don't know how long I'm going to be able to take this. You could cut the tension in this room with a knife. I almost wish Mrs Hill would come in and yell at us or something. Anything, ANYTHING to break this awful silence.

Yes, silence. I know it seems weird that there'd be silence in the G and T room, considering that this is where Boris Pelkowski is supposed to practise his violin, usually with so much vigour that we are forced to lock him in the supply closet so that we are not maddened by the incessant scraping of his bow.

But no. That bow has been silenced . . . I fear forever. Silenced by the cruel blow of heartache, in the form of a philandering girlfriend . . . who happens to be my best friend, Lilly.

Lilly is sitting here next to me pretending like she doesn't feel the waves of silent grief radiating from her boyfriend, who is sitting in the back corner of the room by the globe, his head buried in his arms. She has to be pretending, because everybody else can feel them. The waves of grief emanating from her boyfriend, I mean. At least, I think so. True, Michael is working on his keyboard like nothing is

148

going on. But he has headphones on. Maybe headphones shield you from radiating waves of grief.

I should have asked for headphones for my birthday.

I wonder if I should go over to the Teachers' Lounge and get Mrs Hill and tell her Boris is sick. Because I really do think he might be. Sick, I mean. Sick at heart and possibly even in the brain. How can Lilly be so mean? It is like she is punishing Boris for a crime he didn't commit. All through lunch, Boris kept asking her if they could go somewhere private, like the third-floor stairwell, to talk, and Lilly just kept saying, 'I'm sorry, Boris, but there's nothing to talk about. It's over between us. You're just going to have to accept it, and move on.'

'But why?' Boris kept wailing. Really loud too. Like loud enough that the jocks and cheerleaders, over at the popular people's table, kept looking over at us and sniggering. It was a little embarrassing. But very dramatic. 'What did I do?'

'You didn't do anything,' Lilly said, throwing him a bone at last. 'I am just not in love with you any more. Our relationship has progressed to its natural peak, and while I will always treasure the memories of what we had together it's time for me to move on. I've helped you achieve self-actualization, Boris. You don't need me any more. I have to turn my attention to another tortured soul.'

I don't know what Lilly means about Boris having reached self-actualization. I mean, it isn't like he's got rid of his bionater, or anything. And he's still tucking his sweater into his pants, except when I remind him not to. He is probably the least self-actualized person I know . . .

. . . with the exception of myself, of course.

Boris didn't take any of this too well. I mean, as far as kiss-offs go, it *was* pretty harsh. But Boris should know as well as anybody that once Lilly makes up her mind about something that's pretty much it. She's sitting here right now working on the speech she wants Jangbu to give at a press conference she's having him hold at the Chinatown Holiday Inn tonight.

Boris might as well face it: he's as good as forgotten.

I wonder how the Drs Moscovitz are going to feel when Lilly introduces them to Jangbu. I am fairly sure my dad wouldn't let me date a guy who'd graduated from high school already. Except Michael, of course. But he doesn't count, because I've known him for so long.

Uh-oh. Something is happening. Boris has lifted his head from his desk. He is gazing at Lilly with eyes that remind me of hotly blazing coals . . . if I had ever seen hotly blazing coals, which I haven't, because coal fires are forbidden within the city limits of Manhattan due to anti-smog regulations. But whatever. He is gazing at her with the same kind of fixed concentration he used to stare at his picture of world-class violinist and role model, Joshua Bell. He's opening his mouth. He's about to say something. WHY AM I THE ONLY PERSON IN THIS CLASS WHO IS PAYING THE SLIGHTEST BIT OF ATTENTION TO WHAT IS GOING ON?

Monday. May 5. nurse's office

Oh my God, that was so dramatic I can barely write. Seriously. I have never seen so much blood.

I am almost surely destined for some kind of career in the medical sciences, however, because I didn't feel like fainting. Not even once. In fact, except for Michael and maybe Lars, I think I am the only person in the room to have kept my head. This is undoubtedly due to the fact that, being a writer, I am a natural observer of all human interactions, and I saw what was coming before anyone . . . maybe even Boris. The nurse even said that, if it hadn't been for my quick intervention, Boris might have lost a lot more blood. Ha! How's that for princess-like behaviour, Grandmère? I saved a guy's life!

Well, OK, maybe not his *life*, but, whatever, Boris might have passed out or something if it hadn't been for me. I can't even imagine what caused him to freak out like that. Well, yes, I guess I can. I think the silence in the G and T room caused Boris to go momentarily mental. Seriously.

I can totally see how it would, since it was bugging me as well.

Anyway, what happened was we were all just sitting there, minding our own business — well, except for me, of course, since I was watching Boris — when all of a sudden he stood up and went, 'Lilly, I can't take this any more! You can't do this to me! You've got to give me a chance to prove my undying devotion!'

Or at least it was something like that. It's kind of hard to remember, given what happened next.

I do remember how Lilly replied, however. She was actually somewhat kind. You could tell she felt a little bit bad about her behaviour towards Boris at my party. She went, in a nice voice, 'Boris, seriously, I am so sorry, especially about the way it happened. But the truth is, when a love like mine for Jangbu takes hold, there's no stopping it. You can't hold back New York baseball fans when the Yankees win the World Series. You can't hold back New York shoppers when Century Twenty-One has a sale. You can't hold back the floodwaters in the F train subway tunnels when it pours. Similarly, you can't hold back love like the kind I feel for Jangbu. I am so, so sorry about it, but, seriously, there's nothing I can do. I love him.'

These words, gently as they were spoken — and even I, Lilly's severest critic, with the possible exception of her brother, will admit they were spoken gently — seemed to hit Boris like a fist. He shuddered all over. Next thing I knew, he'd picked up the giant globe next to him — which really was a feat of some athleticism, as that globe weighs a ton. In fact, the reason it's in the G and T room is that it's so heavy, nobody can get it to spin any more, so the administration, rather than throwing it away, must have figured, well, just stick it in the classroom with the nerds, they'll take anything . . . after all, they're nerds.

So there was Boris — hypoglycaemic, asthmatic, deviated-septum and allergy-prone Boris — holding this big heavy globe over his head, as if he were Atlas or He-Man or the Rock or somebody.

'Lilly,' he said in a strangled, very un-Borislike voice — I should probably point out that by this time everyone in the room was paying attention: I mean, Michael had taken off his headphones and was looking at Boris very intently, and even the quiet guy who is supposed to be working on this new kind of superglue that sticks to objects but not to human skin (so you won't have that stuck-together-finger problem any more after gluing up the sole of your shoe) was totally aware of what was happening around him for once.

'If you don't take me back,' Boris said, breathing hard — that globe had to weigh fifty pounds at least, and he was holding it OVER HIS HEAD — 'I will drop this globe on my head.'

Everyone sort of inhaled at the same time. I think I can safely say that there was no doubt in anybody's mind that

Boris meant what he said. He was totally going to drop that globe on his head. Seeing it written down, it looks kind of funny — I mean, really, who DOES things like that? Threatens to drop a globe on his head?

But this WAS Gifted and Talented class. I mean, geniuses are ALWAYS doing weird stuff like dropping globes on their heads. I bet there are geniuses out there who have dropped weirder stuff than globes on their heads. Like cinder blocks and cats and stuff. Just to see what would happen.

I mean, come on. They're geniuses.

Because Boris is a genius, and so is Lilly; she reacted to his threat the way only another genius would. A normal girl, like me, would have gone, 'No, Boris! Put the globe down, Boris! Let's talk, Boris!'

But Lilly, being a genius, and having a genius's curiosity about what would happen if Boris did drop the globe on his head — and maybe because she wanted to see if she really did have enough power over him to make him do it — just went, in a disgusted voice, 'Go ahead. See if I care.'

And that's when it happened. You could tell Boris had second thoughts — like it finally sank into his love-addled brain that dropping a fifty-pound globe on his head probably wasn't the best way to handle the situation.

But just as he was about to put the globe down, it slipped — maybe accidentally. Or maybe on purpose.

What the Drs Moscovitz call a self-fulfilling prophecy, like when you say, 'Oh, I don't want *that* to happen,' and then because you said that and you're thinking about it so much, you accidentally-on-purpose make it happen — and Boris dropped the globe on his head.

The globe made this sickening hollow thunking sound as it hit Boris's skull — the same noise that eggplant made as it hit the pavement that time I dropped it out of Lilly's sixteenth-storey bedroom window — before the whole thing bounced off Boris's head and went crashing to the floor.

And then Boris clapped his hands to his scalp and started staggering around, upsetting the sticky-glue guy, who seemed to be afraid Boris would crash into him and mess up his notes.

It was kind of interesting to see how everyone reacted. Lilly put both hands to her cheeks and just stood there, pale as . . . well, death. Michael swore and started towards Boris. Lars ran from the room, yelling, 'Mrs Hill! Mrs Hill!'

And I — not even really aware of what I was doing — stood up, whipped off my school sweater, strode up to Boris and yelled, 'Sit down!' since he was running all around like a chicken with its head cut off. Not that I have ever seen a chicken with its head recently cut off — I hope never to see this in my lifetime.

But you get what I mean.

156

Boris, to my very great surprise, did what I said. He sank down at the nearest desk, shivering like Rommel during a thunderstorm. Then I said, in the same commanding voice that didn't seem to belong to me, 'Move your hands!'

And Boris moved his hands off his head. That's when I stuck my wadded up sweater over the small hole in Boris's head, to stop the bleeding, just like I saw a vet do on *Animal Precinct* when Officer Anne Marie Lucas brought in a pit bull that had been shot.

After that, all hell — excuse me, but it is true — broke loose.

- Lilly started crying in great big baby sobs, which I haven't seen her do since we were in second grade and I accidentally-on-purpose shoved a spatula down her throat while we were frosting birthday cupcakes to hand out to the class, because she was eating all the frosting and I was afraid there wouldn't be enough to cover all the cupcakes.
- The guy with the glue ran out of the room.
- Mrs Hill came running *into* the room, followed by Lars and about half the faculty, who'd apparently all been in the Teachers' Lounge doing nothing, as the teachers at Albert Einstein High School are wont to do.
- Michael was bent over Boris going, in a calm, soothing

voice I am pretty sure he learned from his parents, who often get calls in the middle of the night from patients of theirs who have gone off their medication for whatever reason and are threatening to drive up and down the Merrick Parkway in a clown suit, 'It's going to be all right. Boris, you're going to be all right. Just take a deep breath. Good. Now take another one. Deep, even breaths. Good. You're going to be fine. You're going to be just fine.'

And I just kept standing there with my sweater pressed to the top of Boris's head, while the globe, having apparently come unstuck thanks to the fall — or perhaps the lubrication from Boris's blood — spun lazily round, eventually coming to rest with the country of Ecuador most prominent.

One of the teachers went and got the nurse, who made me move my sweater a little so that she could see Boris's wound. Then she hastily made me press the sweater back down. Then she said to Boris in the same calming voice Michael was using, 'Come along, young man. Let's go to my office.'

Only Boris couldn't walk to the nurse's office by himself, since when he tried to stand up his knees sort of gave out beneath him, probably on account of his hypoglycaemia. So Lars and Michael half carried Boris to the nurse's office while I just kept my sweater pressed to his head, because, well, nobody had told me to stop.

As we passed Lilly on our way out, I got a good look at her face, and she really had gone pale as death — her face was the colour of New York City snow, kind of pale grey tinged with yellow. She also looked a bit sick to her stomach. Which, if you ask me, serves her right.

So now Michael and Lars and I are sitting here as the nurse fills out an incident report. She called Boris's mother, who is supposed to come get him and take him to their family doctor. While the wound caused by the globe isn't too deep, the nurse thinks it will probably require a few stitches, and that Boris will need a tetanus shot. The nurse was very complimentary of my quick action. She went, 'You're the princess, aren't you?' and I demurely replied that I was.

I can't help feeling really proud of myself.

It is strange how even though I don't like seeing blood in movies and stuff, in real life, it didn't bother me a bit. Seeing Boris's blood, I mean. Because I had to sit with my head between my knees in Bio. that time they showed the acupuncture film. But seeing that blood spurt out of Boris's head in real life didn't cause me so much as a twinge.

Maybe I'll have a delayed reaction, or something. You know, like post-traumatic stress syndrome.

Although, to be frank, if all this princess stuff hasn't caused me PTSS, I highly doubt seeing my best friend's ex-boyfriend drop a globe on his head is going to do it.

Uh-oh. Here comes Principal Gupta.

Monday, May 5, French

Mia, is it true about Boris? Did he really try to kill himself during fifth period by stabbing himself in the chest with a protractor?

> Of course not, Tina. He tried to kill himself by dropping a globe on his head.

OH MY GOD!!!!!!!! Is he going to be all right?

> Yes, thanks to the quick action of Michael and me. He'll probably have a bad headache for a few days, though. The worst part was talking to Principal Gupta. Because of course she wanted to know why he did it. And I didn't want Lilly to get in trouble, or anything. Not that it's Lilly's fault . . . Well, I guess it sort of is . . .

Of course it is!!!!! You don't think she could have handled the whole thing a little better? My God, she was practically Frenching Jangbu right in front of Boris! So what did you say to Principal UpChuck?

161

Oh, you know, the usual. Boris must have cracked under all the pressure AEHS teachers put on us, and why can't the Administration cancel finals like they did in *Harry Potter Two*. Only she didn't listen, because it's not like anyone is dead, or a giant snake was chasing us around, or anything.

Still, it is fully the most romantic thing I have ever heard. Only in my wildest dreams would a man be so desperate to win back my heart that he'd do something like drop a globe on his head.

I know! If you ask me, Lilly is totally rethinking the Jangbu thing. At least, I think so. I actually haven't seen her since it all happened.

My God, who knew that all this time, inside Boris's spindly chest beat the heart of a Heathcliff-like lover?

Tcha! I wonder if his spirit is going to roam around East 75th Street the way Heathcliff's roamed around the moor. You know, after Cathy died.

I kind of always thought Boris was cute. I mean, I know mouth-breathers annoy you, but you have to admit he has very beautiful hands.

HANDS? Who cares about HANDS?????

Um, they are slightly important. Hello. They're what guys TOUCH you with.

You are sick, Tina. Very sick.

Although that might be the pot calling the kettle black, given my whole neck thing with Michael. But whatever. I have never ADMITTED that to anyone. Out loud.

Monday, May 5, in the limo on the way to princess lessons

I am so totally the star of the school. As if the princess thing were not enough, now it's going all around Albert Einstein that Michael and I saved Boris's life. My God, we are like the Dr Kovach and Nurse Abby of AEHS!!!!!!!! And Michael even LOOKS a little like Dr Kovach. You know, with the dark hair and the gorgeous chest and all.

I don't even know why my mother is bothering with a midwife. She should just have me deliver the baby. I could so totally do it. All I'd need is like some scissors and a catcher's mitt. Jeez.

God. I am going to have to rethink this whole writer thing. My talents may lie in a completely different sphere.

Monday, May 5, lobby of the Plaza

Lars just told me that to get into medical school you actually have to have good grades in maths and science. I can see why you'd have to know science, but why MATHS?????? WHY?????? Why is the American educational system conspiring against me to keep me from reaching my career goals?

Monday, May 5, on the way home from the Plaza

Trust Grandmère to burst my bubble. I was still riding high from the medical miracle I'd performed back at school — well, it WAS a miracle: a miracle I hadn't passed out from the sight of all that blood — when Grandmère was like, 'So when can I schedule your fitting at Chanel? Because I've put a dress on hold there that I think will be perfect for this little prom you're so excited about, but if you want it on time, you'll have to have it fitted in the next day or so.'

So then I had to explain to her that Michael and I still weren't going to the prom.

She didn't react to the news like a normal grandmother, of course. A normal grandmother would have been all sympathetic and would have patted my hand and given me some home-baked cookies or a dollar or something.

Not my grandmother. Oh no. *My* grandmother was just like, 'Well, then you obviously didn't do as I instructed.'

Jeez! Blame the victim, Grandma!

'Whaddaya mean?' I blurted out. So of course Grandmère was all, 'What do I mean? Is that what you said? Then ask me properly.'

'What . . . do . . . you . . . mean . . . Grandmère?' I asked her more politely, though inwardly, of course, I didn't feel very polite at all.

'I mean that you haven't done as I said. I told you that, if you found the right incentive, your Michael would be only too happy to escort you to the prom. But clearly you would rather sit around and sulk than take the sort of action necessary to get what it is that you want.'

I took umbrage at that.

'I beg your pardon, Grandmère,' I said, 'but I have done everything humanly possible to convince Michael to go to the prom.' Short, of course, of actually explaining to him *why* it was so important to me to go. Because I'm not so sure that even if I *did* tell Michael why it was so important to me he'd agree to go. And how much would THAT suck? You know, if I bared my soul to the man I love, only to have him decide that his desire not to attend something as lame as the prom was stronger than his desire to see my dream come true?

'On the contrary, you have not,' Grandmère said. She stubbed out her cigarette and, exhaling plumes of grey smoke from her nostrils — it is totally shocking how the weight of the Genovian throne rests solely on my slender shoulders, and yet my own grandmother remains unconcerned about the effects of her second-hand smoke on my lungs — went, 'I've explained this to you before, Amelia. In situations where opposing parties are striving to achieve détente, and yet are failing to reach it, it is always in your best interest to step back and ask yourself what the enemy wants.'

I blinked at her through all the smoke. 'I'm supposed to figure out what Michael wants?'

'Correct.'

I shrugged. 'Easy. He doesn't want to go to the prom. Because it's lame.'

'No. That is what Michael *doesn't* want. What does he *want*?'

I had to think about that one.

'Um,' I said, watching Rommel as he, seeing that Grandmère was otherwise occupied, leaned over and surreptitiously began licking all the fur off one of his paws. 'I guess . . . Michael wants to play in his band?'

'*Bien*,' Grandmère said, which means good in French. 'But what *else* might he want?'

'Um,' I said. 'I don't know.' I was still thinking about the band thing. It is the duty of the freshman, sophomore and junior classes to put on the prom for the seniors, even though we ourselves do not get to go, unless invited by a senior. I tried to remember what the Prom Committee had reported in the *Atom*, so far as the arrangements they'd made for music at the prom. I think they'd hired a DJ or something.

'Of course you know what Michael wants,' Grandmère said sharply. 'Michael wants what *every* man wants.'

'You mean . . . ' I felt stunned by the rapidity with which my grandmother's mind worked. 'You mean I should ask the prom committee to let Michael's band play at the prom?'

Grandmère started to choke for some reason. 'Wh-what?' she demanded, hacking up half a lung, practically.

I sat back in my seat, completely at a loss for words. It had never occurred to me before, but Grandmère's solution to the problem was totally perfect. Nothing would delight Michael more than an actual, paying gig for Skinner Box. And I would get to go to the prom . . . and not just with the man of my dreams, but with *an actual member of the band*. Is there anything cooler in the world than being at the prom with a member of the band playing at the prom? Um, no. No, there is not.

'Grandmère,' I breathed. 'You're a genius!'

Grandmère was slurping up the last of the ice in her Sidecar. 'I don't have the slightest idea what you're talking about, Amelia,' she said.

But I knew that, for the first time in her life, Grandmère was just being modest.

Then I remembered that I was supposed to be angry with her, on account of Jangbu. So I went, 'But, Grandmère, be serious a minute. This thing with the busboys . . . the strike. You've got to do something. It's all your fault, you know.'

Grandmère eyed me over all the blue smoke coming out of the new cigarette she'd just lit.

'Why, you ungrateful little chit,' she said. 'I solve all your problems, and this is the thanks you show me?'

'I'm serious, Grandmère,' I said. 'You've got to call Les Hautes Manger and tell them about Rommel. Tell them it was your fault that Jangbu tripped, and that they've got to hire him back. It isn't fair, otherwise. I mean, the poor guy lost his job!'

'He'll find another,' Grandmère said dismissively.

'Not without references,' I pointed out.

'So he can go back to his native land,' Grandmère said. 'I'm sure his parents miss him.'

'Grandmère, he's from *Tibet*, a country that has been under Chinese oppression for decades. He can't go back there. There are no jobs. He'll starve.'

'I no longer care to discuss this,' Grandmère said loftily. 'Tell me the ten different courses traditionally served at a royal Genovian wedding.'

'Grandmère!'

'Tell me!'

So I had no choice but to rattle off the ten different courses traditionally served at a Genovian wedding — olives, antipasto, pasta, fish, meat, salad, bread, cheese, fruit, dessert (note to self: when Michael and I get married, remember not to do it in Genovia, unless the palace'll do an all-vegetarian meal).

I don't understand how someone who has embraced the dark side as fully as Grandmère can come up with brilliant stuff like getting Michael's band to play at the prom.

But I guess even Darth Vader had his moments. I can't think of any right now, but I'm sure he had some.

Monday, May 5, 9 p.m., the Loft

Bad news:

I spent the whole evening pouring over back issues of the *Atom*, trying to figure out who was head of the Prom Committee, so I could email him/her with my request that Skinner Box be approached as a possible live entertainment alternative to the DJ I know they've got lined up. So you can only imagine my surprise and disappointment when I finally stumbled across the article I was looking for, and saw the horrifying answer right there in black and white:

Lana Weinberger.

LANA WEINBERGER is head of this year's Prom Committee.

Well, that's it. I'm dead. There is NO WAY I'm going to get to go to the prom now. I mean, Lana would sooner go off her Atkins diet than hire my boyfriend's band. I mean, Lana hates my guts, and always has.

And I can't say the feeling isn't mutual.

What am I going to do NOW? I CAN'T miss the prom. I just CAN'T!!!!!!!!!

But I guess I don't have the biggest problems in the world. I mean, there are people with worse ones. Like Boris, for instance. I got this email from him just now:

JoshBell2: Mia, I just wanted to say thanks for what you did for me today. I don't know why I behaved so stupidly. I guess I was just overcome with emotion. I love her so much! But it is clear to me now that we are not destined for one another, as I so long thought (erroneously, I realize at last). No, Lilly is like a wild mustang, born to run free. I see now that no man – least of all someone like me – can ever hope to tame her.

Treasure what you have with Michael, Mia. It is a rare and beautiful thing, to love, and be loved in return.

Boris Pelkowski

PS My mother says she will get your sweater dry-cleaned so I can give it back to you at the end of this week. She says Star Cleaners think they can get the blood out without any permanent staining. B. P.

Poor Boris! Imagine thinking of Lilly as a wild mustang. Wild mushroom, maybe. But a *mustang*? I don't think so.

I figured I'd better check on how she was doing, since last time I'd seen her Lilly'd been looking kind of green around the gills. I sent her a totally non-accusatory, completely friendly email, enquiring into her mental health after her ordeal earlier in the day.

You can imagine my outrage when this is what I got for my efforts:

WomynRule: Hey, P.O.G!

(Pog is the nickname Lilly decided to give me a few weeks ago. It stands for Princess of Genovia. I have asked her repeatedly not to use it but she persists, probably because I made the mistake of letting her know it bugs me.)

Whazzup? Missed you at tonight's SATWDOJPA press conference. Looks like we may actually get the hotel workers' union behind our cause. If we can get hotels 2 strike as well as the restaurant workers, we'll bring the city 2 its knees! Finally, people will start realizing that service industry personnel are not to be messed with! The common man deserves to be paid a living wage!

Wasn't that wild about Boris this afternoon? I have to say, it gave me quite a scare. I had no idea he was such a psycho. Then again, he IS a musician. I should have known. That was pretty cool the way you and Michael handled the situation, tho. You

two were just like Dr McCoy and Nurse Chappell.
Though you'd probably prefer it if I said you were
like Dr Kovach and Nurse Abby. Which I guess you
kind of were. Well, gtg. My mom wants me to put
the dishes away.
Lil

PS Jangbu did the sweetest thing after the press
conference tonight: he bought me a silk rose from a
booth on Canal Street. Soooo romantic. Boris never
did stuff like that. L

I have to admit: I was shocked. Shocked by Lilly's cavalier
dismissal of poor Boris's pain. Shocked by her *whazzup* and
her reference to the original *Star Trek*, which if *I'd* used
Lilly would have rebuked me for being passé, the original
Star Trek hardly being on the cutting edge of pop culture.
And REALLY shocked at her implication that all musicians
are psychos. I mean, hello! Her brother, Michael, MY
BOYFRIEND, is a musician! And, yes, we certainly have our
problems, but not because he is in any way a psycho. In
fact, if anything, my problems with Michael have to do with
the fact that he, as a Capricorn, has his feet planted TOO
firmly on the ground, whereas I, a free-wheeling Taurus,
want to bring a little more fun into our relationship.

I wrote back to her right away. I will admit I was so angry, my hands were shaking as I typed.

FtLouie: Lilly, it might interest you to know that Boris had to get two stitches AND a tetanus shot because of what happened in G and T today. Furthermore, he might even have concussion. Perhaps you could tear yourself away from your tireless work on behalf of Jangbu, a guy YOU ONLY MET THREE DAYS AGO, and spare a little sympathy for your ex, whom you dated for EIGHT WHOLE MONTHS.
M

Lilly's response was almost instantaneous.

WomynRule: Excuse me, P.O.G., but I can't say I really appreciate your condescending tone. Kindly don't pull your Royal Highness act on me. I'm sorry if you don't happen to like Jangbu or the work I am doing to help him and people like him. However, that does not mean I need to be held hostage to my old relationship by the juvenile theatrics of a self-delusional narcissist like Boris. I did not make him pick up that globe and drop it on his head.

He made that choice all on his own. I would think you, as a faithful viewer of the Lifetime Movie Channel for Women, would recognize manipulative behaviour like Boris's as classic stalker stuff.

But then, maybe if you stopped watching so many movies, and actually tried living life for a change, you might recognize this. You also might be writing something a little bit more challenging for the school paper than the cafeteria beat.

I could tell she was feeling guilty over what she'd done to Boris by how thoroughly she attacked him. That I could ignore. But her attack on my writing could not go unnoticed. I immediately fired back with:

FtLouie: Yeah, well, I may watch a lot of movies, but at least I don't go around with my face glued to a camera lens, the way you do. I prefer to WATCH movies not invent drama FOR the movies. Furthermore, I will have you know that Lesley Cho asked me to cover a hard news story for the paper just the other day.

This is what I just got in reply.

WomynRule: Yeah, a story *I* made possible. You are so weak. Go back to pining over the fact that you have to spend your summer in a palace in Genovia (wah-wah-wah) and that my brother doesn't want to go to the prom with you, and leave the REAL problem-solving to people like me, who are better equipped intellectually to handle it.

Well, that's the last straw. Lilly Moscovitz is no longer my best friend. I have taken all the abuse I can stand. I am thinking about writing back to her to tell her that.

But maybe that would be too childish, and not INTELLECTUAL enough.

Maybe I'll just ask Tina if she'll be my best friend from now on.

But no, that would be too childish too. I mean, it's not like we're in third grade any more. We're practically women, like my mom said. Women like my mom don't go around declaring who is their best friend and who isn't. They just sort of . . . know. Without saying anything about it. I don't know how, but they do. Maybe it is an oestrogen thing, or something.

Oh my God, I have such a headache.

Monday, May 5, 11 p.m.

I almost burst into tears just now when I checked my email one last time before bed. That's because this is what I found there:

LinuxRulz: Mia, are you sure you aren't mad at me about something? Because you hardly said three words to me all day. Except during the whole Boris thing. Did I do something wrong?

Then another one, a second later:

LinuxRulz: Nevermind that last email. It was stupid. I know if I'd done something to upset you, you'd have told me. Because that's the kind of girl you are. That's one of the reasons we're so good together. Because we can tell each other anything.

Then:

LinuxRulz: It's not that thing from your party, is it? You know, where I wouldn't beat up Jangbu for making out with my sister? Because getting involved in my sister's love life is never a good idea, as you might have noticed.

Then:

LinuxRulz: Well, whatever. Goodnight. And I love you.

Oh, Michael! My sweet protector!
WHY WON'T YOU TAKE ME TO YOUR PROM????????
?????????????????????

Tuesday, May 6, 3 a.m.

I still can't believe the nerve of her. I have learned A LOT about writing from watching movies. For instance:

Valuable tips I, Mia Thermopolis, learned about writing from the movies:

Aspen Extreme

T. J. Burke moves to Aspen to become a ski instructor, but really he just wants to write. When he is done penning his touching tribute to his dead friend, Dex, he puts it in an envelope and sends it to *Powder* magazine. A hot-air balloon and two swans fly by. Then you see a mail carrier put a copy of *Powder* magazine in T.J.'s mailbox. On the cover is a blurb about T.J.'s story! It's that easy to get published!

The Wonderboys

Always keep a back-up disk.

Little Women

Ditto.

Moulin Rouge

When writing a play, do not fall in love with your leading lady. Especially if she has consumption. Also, don't drink anything green offered to you by a midget.

The Bell Jar

Don't let your mother read your book until *after* it's published (when there's nothing she can do about it).

Adaptation

Never trust a twin.

Isn't She Great, The Jacqueline Suzann Story

Publishers don't actually mind if you turn in a manuscript written on pink stationery. Also, sex sells.

How DARE Lilly suggest I've wasted my time watching TV?

And if I happen to choose a career in the medical profession I am still golden, because I have seen practically every episode of *ER* ever made.

Not to mention *M*A*S*H*.

Tuesday, May 6, Gifted and Talented

Horrible day so far, in every way:

1. Mr G gave us a pop quiz in Algebra, which I flunked because I was too worked up over the whole Boris/Lilly/prom thing last night to study. You would think my own stepfather would be kind enough to drop me a hint or two when he's going to give a pop quiz. But apparently this would violate some teacher code of ethics.

As if. What about the stepfather code of ethics? Anyone ever thought about THAT?

2. Shameeka and I got caught passing notes again. Have to write a thousand-word essay on effects of global warming on ecosystems of South America.

3. I had no one to be my partner on the disease projects we are doing in Health and Safety because Lilly and I aren't speaking. She is doing the full-on avoidance thing. She even took the subway to school today instead of riding with Michael and me in the limo. Not that I mind. Plus when we drew diseases I got Asperger's syndrome. Why couldn't I have got a cool disease, like Ebola fever? It is

so unfair, especially as I am now considering a career in the health field.

4. At lunch I accidentally ate some sausage that was mistakenly baked into my supposedly cheese-only Individual Pizza. Also, Boris spent the whole period writing the word *Lilly* over and over again on his violin case. Lilly didn't even show at lunch. Hopefully she and Jangbu hopped a plane back to Tibet and won't be bothering any of us any more. Michael says he doesn't think so, though. He says he thinks she had another press conference.

5. Michael did not change his mind about the prom. Not that I brought it up, or anything. Just that I happened to be walking with him past the table where Lana and the rest of the Prom Committee are selling tickets, and Michael went, "Sucka," under his breath when he saw the guy who hates it when they put corn in the chilli buying prom tickets for himself and his girlfriend.

Even the guy who hates it when they put corn in the chilli is going to the prom. Everyone in the whole world is going to the prom. Except for me.

Lilly still isn't back from wherever it is she went off to before lunch. Which is probably just as well. I don't think

Boris could take it if she walked in here right now. He found some correcting fluid in the supply closet, and he is using it to make little curlicues around Lilly's name on his violin case. I want to shake him and go, 'Snap out of it! She's not worth it!'

But I'm afraid it might loosen his stitches.

Plus Mrs Hill, clearly due to yesterday's events, is fully sitting at her desk, flipping through Garnet Hill catalogues and keeping an eagle eye on us. I bet she got in trouble over the whole violin-virtuoso-globe-dropping thing. Principal Gupta is really very strict about bloodshed on school grounds.

Since I have nothing better to do, I am going to compose a poem that expresses my true feelings about everything that is going on. I intend to call it *Spring Fever*. If it is good enough, I am going to submit it to the *Atom*. Anonymously, of course. If Lesley knew I wrote it, she'd never print it, since, as a cub reporter, I have not Paid My Dues.

But if she just FINDS it slipped under the door to the *Atom's* office, maybe she'll run it. The way I see it, I have nothing to lose. It's not like things can possibly get any worse.

Tuesday, May 6, St Vincent's Hospital

Things just got worse. Very, very worse.

It's probably all my fault. All my fault because I wrote that before. About things not possibly being able to get any worse. It turns out things most definitely CAN get worse than

- Flunking an Algebra quiz
- Getting in trouble in Bio. for passing notes
- Getting Asperger's syndrome as your Health and Safety project
- Your father trying to force you to spend most of your summer in Genovia
- Your boyfriend refusing to take you to the prom
- Your best friend calling you weak
- Her boyfriend needing stitches in his head from a self-inflicted globe wound
- Your grandmother trying to force you to have dinner with the Sultan of Brunei

What's worse is your pregnant mother passing out in the frozen-food department at the Grand Union.

I am totally serious. She landed face first in the Häagen

Dazs. Thank God she bounced off the Ben and Jerry's and came to rest on her back, or my potential brother or sister would have been crushed under the weight of his or her own mother.

The manager of the Grand Union apparently didn't have the slightest idea what to do. According to witnesses, he ran all around the store, flapping his arms and yelling, 'Dead woman in Aisle Four! Dead woman in Aisle Four!'

I don't know what would have happened if members of the New York Fire Department hadn't happened to have been there. I'm serious. Ladder Company Number 3 does all its grocery shopping for the firehouse at the Grand Union — I know because Lilly and I, back when we were friends and first realized firemen are hot, used to go there all the time to watch them as they picked through the nectarines and mangoes — and they happened to be there stocking up for the week when my mom went horizontal. They checked her pulse right away and figured out she wasn't dead. Then they called an ambulance and whisked her to St Vincent's, the closest ER.

Too bad my mom was unconscious the whole time. She would so totally have loved to have ridden in an ambulance with all those hot guys. Plus, you know, the fact that they were strong enough to lift her . . . and at her current weight, which is a lot . . . that's pretty cool.

You can imagine when I was just sitting there, bored out of my skull in French, and my mobile phone rang . . . well, I freaked. Not because it was the first time anyone had ever called me, or even because Mademoiselle Klein fully confiscates any mobile phones that ring during her class, but because the only people who are allowed to call me on my mobile phone are my mom and Mr G, and then only to let me know that I need to get to home, because my sibling is about to be born.

Except that when I finally answered the phone — it took me a minute to figure out it was MY phone that was ringing: I kept looking around accusingly at everybody else in class, who just blinked confusedly back at me — it wasn't my mom or Mr G to tell me the baby was coming. It was Assistant Fire Chief Pete Logan, to ask me if I knew a Helen Thermopolis and, if so, could I come to St Vincent's hospital immediately. The firemen had found my mom's mobile phone in her bag, and dialled the only number she had in her address book . . .

Mine.

I about had a coronary, of course. I shrieked and grabbed my backpack, then Lars. Then he and I ran out of there without a word of explanation to anyone . . . like I had suddenly developed Asperger's syndrome or something. On our way out of the building, I skidded past Mr Gianini's classroom, then backed up and stuck my head in to scream that his wife was in the hospital and that he better put down that chalk and come with us.

I've never seen Mr G look so scared. Not even the first time he met Grandmère.

Then the three of us ran all out for the 77th Street subway station — because there was no way a cab was going to get us there fast enough in the midday traffic, and Hans and the limo are off duty every day until I get out of school at three.

I don't think the staff at St Vincent — who are totally excellent, by the way — ever encountered anything quite like a hysterical Princess of Genovia, her bodyguard and her stepfather before. The three of us burst into the ER waiting area and just stood there screaming my mom's name until finally this nurse came out of triage and was like, 'Helen Thermopolis is just fine. She's awake and resting right now. She just got a little dehydrated, and fainted.'

'Dehydrated?' I about had another coronary, but this time for different reasons. 'She hasn't been drinking her eight glasses of water a day?'

The nurse smiled and said, 'Well, she mentioned that the baby is putting a lot of pressure on her bladder . . . '

'Is she going to be all right?' Mr G wanted to know.

'Is the BABY going to be all right?' I wanted to know.

'Both of them are going to be fine,' the nurse said. 'Come with me, and I'll take you to her.'

Then the nurse took us into the ER — the actual ER of St Vincent's Hospital, where everybody in Greenwich Village who gets shot or has a kidney stone goes!!!!!!!!!!! I saw tons of sick people in there. There was a guy who had all sorts of tubes sticking out of him, and another guy who was throwing up in a basin. There was an NYU student 'sleeping one off', and an old lady who'd had heart palpitations, and a supermodel who'd fallen off her stilettos, and a construction worker who had a gash on his hand and a bike messenger who had been hit by a taxi.

Anyway, before I got a good look at all the patients — patients like the ones I might have some day, if I ever pull up my Algebra grades and get into medical school — the nurse tugged a curtain back, and there was my mom, awake and looking pretty peeved.

When I noticed the needle in her arm, I saw why she was so peeved. She was hooked up to an IV!!!!!!!!!!!!!

'OH MY GOD!!!' I yelled at the nurse. Even though you aren't supposed to yell in the ER, because there are sick people there. 'If she's so OK, why does she have THAT???'

'It's just to get some fluids into her,' the nurse said. 'Your mom is going to be fine. Tell them you're going to be fine, Mrs Thermopolis.'

'It's *Ms*,' my mom snarled.

And I knew then that she was going to be just fine.

I threw myself on her and gave her the biggest hug I could, what with the IV and the fact that Mr G was hugging her too.

'I'm all right, I'm all right,' my mom said, patting us both on our heads. 'Let's not make a bigger deal out of this than has been made already.'

'But it IS a big deal,' I said, feeling tears trickle down my face. Because it is very upsetting, getting a phone call in the middle of French class from an assistant fire chief, telling you that your mother is in hospital.

'No, it's not,' my mom said. 'I'm fine. The baby's fine. And once they get the rest of this Ringer's lactate into me I get to go home.' She shot the nurse a look. 'RIGHT?'

'Yes, ma'am,' the nurse said, and closed the curtain so that the four of us — my mom, Mr G, me and my bodyguard — could have some privacy. 'You have to be more careful, Mom,' I said. 'You can't let yourself get worn out like this.'

'I'm not worn out,' my mom said. 'It's that damned roast pork and noodle soup I had for lunch—'

'From Number One Noodle Son?' I cried, horrified. 'Mom, you didn't! There's like one million grammes of sodium in that! No wonder you passed out! The MSG alone—'

191

'I have an idea, Your Highness,' Lars said, speaking in a low voice in my ear. 'Why don't you and I go across the street and see if we can get your mother a smoothie?'

Lars always keeps such a level head in a crisis. That is no doubt on account of his intensive training with the Israeli Army. He is a distinguished expert marksman with his Glock, and pretty good with a flamethrower too. Or so he once confided in me.

'That's a good idea,' I said. 'Mom, Lars and I will be right back. We're going to get you a nice, healthy smoothie.'

'Thanks,' my mom said weakly, but for some reason she was looking more at Lars than at me. No doubt because her eyes were still out of focus from the whole fainting thing.

Except that when we returned with the smoothie, the nurse wouldn't let us back in to see my mom. She said there was only one visitor per hour per patient in the ER, and that she'd only made an exception before because we'd all looked so worried and she'd wanted us to see for ourselves that Mom was OK, and I'm the Princess of Genovia, and all.

She did take the smoothie Lars and I had bought, and promised to give it to my mom.

So now Lars and I are sitting in the hard orange plastic chairs in the waiting room. We'll be here until my mom gets dismissed. I already called Grandmère and cancelled my princess lesson for the day. I must say, Grandmère wasn't very alarmed, once she heard my mom was going to be all right. You would think relatives of hers faint in the Grand Union every day. My dad's reaction to the news was much more gratifying. He got ALL worked up and wanted to fly in the royal physician all the way from Genovia to make sure the baby's heartbeat was regular and that the pregnancy wasn't putting undue stress on my mom's admittedly worn-out thirty-six-year-old system——

OH MY GOD!!!!!!!!!! You'll never guess who just walked into the ER. My OWN royal consort, HRH Michael Moscovitz Renaldo to be.

More later.

Tuesday, May 6, the Loft

Michael is SO sweet!!!!!!!!! As soon as school let out he rushed over to the hospital to make sure my mom was all right. He found out what happened from my dad. Can you IMAGINE???? He was so worried when he heard from Tina that I had gone rushing out of French that he called MY DAD when he couldn't get an answer at the Loft.

How many boys would willingly call their girlfriend's dad? Hmmm? None that I know of. Especially if their girlfriend's dad happened to be a crowned PRINCE, like my dad. Most boys would be too scared to call their girlfriend's dad in a situation like that.

But not *my* boyfriend.

Too bad he still thinks the prom is lame. But whatever. Having your pregnant mother pass out in the refrigerated section of the Grand Union has a way of putting things into perspective.

And now I know that, much as I would have loved to have gone, the prom is not really important. What is important is family togetherness, and being with the ones you love, and being blessed with good health and—

Oh, God, what am I talking about? Of COURSE I still want to go the prom. Of COURSE it's still killing me inside that Michael refuses even to entertain the IDEA of going.

I fully brought it up right there in the St Vincent's ER waiting room. I was helped, of course, by the fact that there's a TV in the waiting room, and that the TV was turned to CNN, and that CNN was doing a story on proms and the trends towards separate proms in many urban high schools — you know, like one prom for the white kids, who dance around to Eminem, and one prom for the African-American students, who dance around to Ashanti.

Only at Albert Einstein, there is only one prom, because Albert Einstein is a school that promotes cultural diversity and plays both Eminem *and* Ashanti at its events.

So since we were still waiting for my mom to get through with her Ringer's lactate, and we were all three of us just sitting there — me, Michael, and Lars — watching the TV and the occasional ambulance that came rolling in, bringing yet another patient to the ER, I went, to Michael, 'Come on. Doesn't that look like fun?'

Michael, who was watching the ambulance and not the TV, went, 'Getting your chest cracked open with a rib spreader in the middle of Seventh Avenue? Not really.'

'No,' I said. 'On the TV. You know. Prom.'

Michael looked up at the TV, at all the students dancing in their formal wear, and went, 'No.'

'Yeah, but seriously. Think about it. It might be cool. You know. To go and make fun of.' This was not really my idea of a perfect prom night, but it was better than nothing. 'And you don't have to wear a tux, you know. I mean, there's like no rule that says you do. You could just wear a suit. Or not even a suit. You could wear jeans and one of those T-shirts that *look* like a tux.'

Michael looked at me like he thought I might have dropped a globe on my head.

'You know what would be even more fun?' he said. '*Bowling.*'

I heaved this enormous sigh. It was sort of hard to have this intensely personal conversation there in the St Vincent's ER waiting room, because not only was my bodyguard sitting RIGHT THERE, but so were all these sick people, some of whom were coughing EXTREMELY loudly right in my ear.

But I tried to remember the fact that I am a gifted healer and should be tolerant of their disgusting germs.

'But, Michael,' I said. 'Seriously. We could go bowling any old night. And frequently do. Wouldn't it be more fun, just once, to get all dressed up and go dancing?'

'You want to go dancing?' Michael perked up. 'We could go dancing. We could go to the Rainbow Room if you want. My parents go there on their anniversary and stuff. It's supposed to be really nice. There's live music, really great old-time jazz, and——'

'Yeah,' I said. 'I know. I'm sure the Rainbow Room is very nice. But I mean, wouldn't it be nice to go dancing some place with PEOPLE OUR OWN AGE?'

'Like from AEHS?' Michael looked sceptical. 'I guess so. I mean, if like Trevor and Felix and Paul were going to be there . . . ' These are the guys from his band. 'But, you know, they wouldn't be caught dead at something as lame as the prom.'

OH MY GOD. It is EXTREMELY hard to be lifemates with a musician. Talk about marching to your own drummer. Michael marches to his own BAND.

I know Michael and Trevor and Felix and Paul are cool and all, but I still fail to see what is so lame about the prom. I mean, you get to elect a Prom King and Queen. At what other social function do you get to elect monarchs to rule over the proceedings? Hello, how about none.

But whatever. I am not going to let Michael's refusal to act like a typical male seventeen-year-old get in the way of my enjoyment of this evening. You know, the family togetherness my mom and Mr G and I are currently having. We are all having a nice time watching *Miracle Pets*. An old lady had a heart attack and her pet pig walked TWENTY miles to get help.

Fat Louie wouldn't walk to the corner to get help for me. Or he might, but he would soon be distracted by a pigeon and run off, never to be seen again, while my corpse rotted on the floor.

Asperger's Syndrome

A Report by
Mia Thermopolis

The condition known as Asperger's syndrome (also known as pervasive developmental disorder) is marked by an inability to function normally in social interactions with others (wait a minute . . . this sounds like . . . ME!).

The person suffering from Asperger's exhibits poor non-verbal communication skills (oh my God – this is ME!!!!!!!!!), is unsuccessful in developing relationships with peers (also me), is incapable of expressing pleasure in the happiness of others (wait – this is totally Lilly), and does not react appropriately in social situations (ME ME ME!!!!!!!). There is a higher incidence of the syndrome in males (OK, not me). Frequently, sufferers of Asperger's syndrome are socially inept (ME). When tested, however, many score in the above average intelligence range (OK, not me – but Lilly, definitely) and will often excel in fields like science, computer programming and music (oh my God! Michael! No! Not Michael! Anyone but Michael!).

Symptoms may include:

- *Abnormal non-verbal communication – problems with eye contact, facial expressions, body postures or uncontrolled gesturing (ME! Also Boris!).*

- *Inability to develop relationships with peers (totally me. Also Lilly).*

- *Labelled by other children as 'weird' or 'freakish' (this is creeping me out!!! Lana calls me a freak nearly every day!!!).*

- *Atypical or noticeably impaired expression of pleasure in other people's happiness (LILLY!!!! She is NEVER happy for ANYONE!!!!!!).*

- *Lack of response to social or emotional feelings (LILLY!!!!!!).*

- *Inability to be flexible regarding minor trivialities, such as alterations to specific routines or rituals (Grandmère!!!!!! ALSO MY DAD!!!!!!! Also Lars. And Mr G).*

- *Continuous or repetitive finger tapping, hand wringing, knee jiggling or whole body movements (well, this is totally Boris, as anyone who has ever seen him play Bartók on his violin could attest).*

- *Obsessive interest or concern with subjects such as world history, rock collecting or plane schedules (or possibly — PROM????????? Does being obsessed with the prom count? Oh my God, I have Asperger's syndrome! I totally have Asperger's!!!! But wait. If I have it, so does Lilly. Because she is obsessed with Jangbu Pinasa. And Boris is obsessed with his violin. And Tina with romance novels. And Michael with his band. Oh my GOD!!!!!!!! We ALL have Asperger's syndrome!!!!!!!! This is terrible. I wonder if Principal Gupta knows???????? Wait . . . what if AEHS is a special Asperger's syndrome school? And none of us know it? Until now, that is . . . I am going to bust the whole thing wide open! Like Woodward and Bernstein! Mia Thermopolis, forging a path for Asperger's sufferers everywhere!).*

- *Obsessive concern or attention to parts of objects rather than the whole (I don't know what this means, but it sounds like ME!!!!!!!!).*

- *Repetitive behaviours, generally self-injurious in nature (BORIS!!!!!!! Dropping globes on his head!!!!!!!!! But wait, he only did that once . . .).*

Symptoms not included in Asperger's:

* No indication of language retardation (duh. We are all excellent talkers) or of retardation in typical age-appropriate curiosity (seriously. I mean, Lilly got to second base already and she is only in the ninth grade).

First identified in 1944 as 'autistic psychopathy' by Hans Asperger, the cause of this disorder is still unknown. Asperger's syndrome may possibly be related to autism. There is no known cure for Asperger's at this time and, indeed, some case subjects do not consider the disorder an impairment at all. To eliminate other causes, physical, emotional and mental evaluations are usually administered to suspected cases of Asperger's.

Lilly, Michael, Boris, Tina and I ALL need to take these tests!!!!! Oh my God, we've had Asperger's all along and never knew!!!! I wonder if Mr Wheeton knows, and that's why he assigned me this condition!!!!! This is spooky . . .

Tuesday, May 6, the Loft

I just went into my mother's bedroom (Mr G is on an emergency run to Grand Union to secure more Häagen-Dazs for her) and demanded to know the truth about my mental health status.

'Mother,' I said. 'Am I, or am I not, a sufferer of Asperger's syndrome?'

My mom was trying to watch a bunch of episodes of *Charmed* she'd recorded. She says *Charmed* is actually a very feminist show because it portrays young women who fight evil without the help of males, but I notice that a) they often fight while wearing halter tops, and b) my mother takes a special interest in the episodes where men take their shirts off.

But whatever. In any case, her reply to me was way cranky.

'For God's sake, Mia,' she said. 'Are you doing another report for Health and Safety?'

'Yes,' I said. 'And it is clear to me that you have been hiding from everyone the fact that I am a sufferer of Asperger's syndrome, and that, in fact, you send me to a special school for Asperger's sufferers. And the lying has got to stop now!'

She just looked at me and went, 'Are you seriously trying to tell me that you don't remember last month, when you were convinced you had Tourette's syndrome?'

I protested that this was totally different. Tourette's is a disorder characterized by multiple motor and vocal tics that begin prior to the age of eighteen, and at the time we were studying it in class, my constant use of words such as 'like' and 'totally' seemed totally characteristic of the disease.

Is it my fault that generally the tics are accompanied by involuntary bodily movements, from which I apparently don't suffer?

'Are you trying to say,' I demanded, 'that I don't have Asperger's syndrome?'

'Mia,' my mother said. 'There is nothing wrong with you. You are one hundred per cent Asperger's syndrome-free.

I couldn't believe this, however, after everything I'd read.

'Are you SURE?' I asked. 'What about Lilly?'

My mom snorted. 'Well. I wouldn't go so far as to say that Lilly is normal. But I highly doubt she is suffering from Asperger's.'

Damn! I wish she were. Lilly, I mean. Because then I might be able to forgive her. For calling me weak, I mean.

But as she has no disease there is no excuse for the way she's treated me.

I have to admit, I'm a little sad I don't have Asperger's.

Because now my obsession with the prom is just that: my obsession with the prom. And not a symptom of a disease over which I have no control.

Just my luck!

Wednesday, May 7, 3:30 a.m.

I realize now what I am going to have to do. I mean, I think I knew it all along, and I was just blocking it. Which isn't surprising, considering that every fibre of my being is crying out against it.

But really, what choice do I have? Michael himself even said it: he'd go to the prom if the guys from his band were going too.

Oh, God, I can't believe it has come to this. My life really IS going down the toilet if this is the low to which I am forced to stoop.

I'll never be able to get to sleep now. I just know it. I am too filled with dread.

The Atom

The Official Student-Run Newspaper of
Albert Einstein High School

Take *Pride* in the AEHS Lions

Week of May 12   *Volume 456/Issue 28*

Notice to all Students:
As we enter final exams in the next few weeks, school administrators would like us to review the AEHS mission statement and beliefs:

Mission Statement

It is Albert Einstein High School's mission to provide students with learning experiences that are technologically relevant, globally orientated and personally challenging.

Beliefs:
1. The school must provide a diverse curriculum that includes a strong academic programme enhanced by numerous electives.
2. A well-supported and diverse extra-curricular programme is an essential supplement to the academic programme in helping students explore a wide range of interests and abilities.
3. Students must be encouraged to develop responsible behaviour and accountability for their actions.
4. Tolerance and understanding of different cultures and viewpoints must be encouraged at all times.
5. Cheating or plagiarism will not be condoned in any form, and can lead to suspension or expulsion.

The administration would like the student body to be aware that in the coming exam period, it intends to enforce point 5 with vigilance. Forewarned is forearmed.

Incident at Les Hautes Manger
by Mia Thermopolis

Having been asked by this paper to provide an account of what occurred last week at the restaurant Les Hautes Manger, at which this reporter was present, it must be noted that the entire thing was the fault of this reporter's grandmother, who smuggled her dog into the restaurant. The said dog's ill-timed break for freedom caused busboy Jangbu Pinasa to drop a soup-laden tray on to the Dowager Princess of Genovia's person.

The consequent dismissal of Jangbu Pinasa was both unfair and possibly unconstitutional. Though this reporter isn't sure, due to her lack of familiarity with said constitution. It is this reporter's feeling that Mr Pinasa should be given his job back.

Editorial

While it is not the policy of this paper to print anonymous submissions, the following poem so neatly sums up what so many of us are feeling at this time of year that we decided to run it anyway. – Ed.

Spring Fever
By Anonymous

Sneaking away during lunch – Taco salad, the kind with the meat in it, and the Green Goddess dressing. God, why do they do that to us?

We find that Central Park beckons – Green grass and daffodils pushing their way out from underneath a blanket of cigarette butts and crumpled soda cans.

So we make a run for it – Did they see us? I don't think so. Can we get In-School suspension for a first offence? I guess anything is possible. Let's sit on the bench and try to get a tan . . .
Only to find, to our dismay, that we've left our sunglasses back in our lockers.

Please note:

It is the policy of this administration to suspend any and all students who leave campus during school hours for WHATEVER REASON. Spring Fever is not an acceptable excuse for violating this school policy.

Student Injured by Globe
by Melanie Greenbaum

An AEHS student suffered an in-class injury yesterday due to a large globe that fell, or was dropped on his head. If it was the latter, this reporter feels it necessary to ask: where was the adult supervision at the time said globe was dropped? And if it was the former, why is this administration allowing dangerous objects such as globes to be placed at heights from which they might fall and cause injury to our students? This reporter demands a thorough investigation.

Letters to the Editor:

To Whom it May Concern:
The amount of malaise evidenced by the student body of this establishment is a personal embarrassment to me and a disgrace to our generation. While the students of Albert Einstein High School sit around, planning their Senior Prom and whining about their finals, people in Tibet are DYING. Yes, DYING. Clashes continue between the rebels and the Chinese military, making it impossible for many Tibetans to make even a meagre living.

But what is our government doing to help the people of Tibet? Nothing more than advising tourists to stay away. People, the Tibetans make their *living* from tourists who come to climb the Himalayas. Please do not listen to our government's warnings to avoid Tibet. Encourage your parents to allow you to vacation there this summer – you'll be glad you did.
Lilly Moscovitz

AEHS Food Court Menu
compiled by Mia Thermopolis

Monday	Tuesday	Wednesday	Thursday	Friday
Spicy Chix	Nachos Deluxe	Italian Beef	Fish Stix	Italian Beef
Meatball Sub	Indiv. Pizza	Deli Bar	Pasta Bar	Buffalo Bites
Fr. Bread Pizza	Chicken Pattie	Burrito	Chicken Parm	Grilled Cheese
Potato Bar	Soup & Sand.	Taco Salad Bar	Asian Bar	Bean Bar
Fish Fingers	Tuna in Pitta	Corndog/Pickle	Corn/FF	Curly Fries

Take out your own
personal ad! Available to AEHS students at 50 cents/line

Happy Ad
Shop at Ho's Deli for all your school supply needs! New this week: PAPER, BINDER CLIPS, TAPE. Also Yu-Gi-Oh cards, Slimfast

---

For Sale:
One Fender precision bass, baby-blue, never been played. With amp, how-to guides. Best Offer. Locker No. 345

Looking for Love:
Female frosh, loves romance/reading, wants older boy who enjoys same. Must be taller than 5'8", no mean people, non-smokers only, musician preferred. no metalheads, nice hands a must.
Email: Iluvromance@aehs.edu

Happy Ad
Personal to from BP to LM – I'm sorry for what I did, but I want you to know that I still love you. PLEASE meet me by my locker after school today and allow me to express my devotion to you. Lilly, you are my muse. Without you, the music is gone. please don't let our love die this way.

Wednesday, May 7, Algebra

Well, I did it. I can't say it went over very well — in fact, it did not go over AT ALL well. But I did it. No one can say I didn't do EVERYTHING POSSIBLE to try to get my boyfriend to take me to his prom.

Oh, God, but WHY did it have to be LANA WEINBERGER???? WHY???? I mean, ANYBODY else — Melanie Greenbaum, even. But no. It had to be Lana. I had to grovel to LANA WEINBERGER.

Oh, God, my skin is still crawling.

She was so not receptive to my offer, either. You would have thought I was asking her to strip naked and sing the school song in the middle of lunch (no, wait — Lana probably wouldn't mind doing that).

I got to class early, because I know Lana usually likes to get there before the second bell to make a few calls on her mobile. There she was, all right, the only person in the room, yakking away to someone named Sandy about her prom dress — she really did get a black off-one-shoulder one with a butterfly hem from Nicole Miller (I so hate her). Anyway, I went up to her — which I think was VERY brave of me considering every time I fall under Lana's radar she makes some catty personal remark about my physical appearance. But whatever. I just stood there next to her desk while she yammered into the phone, until she finally realized I wasn't going away. Then she went, 'Hold on a minute, will you, Sandy? There's a . . . *person* who wants something.' Then she held the phone away from her face, looked up at me with those big baby blues of hers, and went, 'WHAT?'

'Lana,' I said. I swear, I have sat next to the Emperor of Japan, OK? I once shook the hand of Prince Harry. I even stood next to Imelda Marcos in line for the ladies' room at *The Producers*. But none of those events ever made me as nervous as Lana does with a mere glance. Because of course Lana has made tormenting me a special personal hobby of hers. That kind of terror runs deeper than the fear of meeting emperors or princes or dictators'wives.

'Lana,' I said again, trying to get my voice to stop shaking. 'I need to ask you something.'

'No,' Lana said, and got back on to her mobile.

'I haven't even asked you yet,' I cried.

'Well, the answer is still no,' Lana said, tossing around her shiny blonde hair. 'Now, where was I? Oh yes, so I am fully getting body glitter and putting it on my — no, not *there*, Sandy! You are so *bad*.'

'It's just . . .' I had to talk fast because, of course, there was a strong chance Michael was going to stop by the

Algebra classroom on his way to AP English, as he does almost every day. I did not want him to know what I was up to. '. . . I know you're on the Prom Committee, and I really think this year's senior class deserves live music at their prom, and not just a DJ. That's why I was thinking you should ask Skinner Box to play.'

Lana went, 'Hold on, Sandy. That *person* still hasn't gone away.' Then she looked at me from between her thickly mascaraed eyelashes and went, '*Skinner Box*? You mean that band of geeks who played that stupid princess-of-my-heart song to you on your birthday?'

I said, taking umbrage, 'Excuse me, Lana, but you shouldn't speak so disparagingly of geeks. If it were not for geeks, we would not have computers, or vaccinations against many major diseases, or antibiotics, or even that mobile you are talking into—'

'Yeah,' Lana said briskly. 'Whatever. The answer is still no.'

Then she went back to her phone conversation.

I stood there for a minute, feeling colour rush into my face. I must really be making progress with my impulse control, since I didn't reach out and grab her mobile from her and crush it beneath my Doc Martens as I might once have. Being the proud owner of a mobile phone myself now, I know just how completely heinous doing something like that would be. Also, you know, considering how much trouble I got into the last time I did it.

Instead, I just stood there with my cheeks burning and my heart beating really fast and my breath coming out in these shallow little gasps. It seems like no matter what kind of strides I make in the rest of my life — you know, behaving with level-headed calmness in medical emergencies; knighting people; almost getting to second base with my boyfriend — I still can't seem to figure out how to act around Lana. I just don't get why she hates me so much. I mean, what did I ever DO to her? Nothing.

Well, except for the whole mobile-phone-stomping thing. Oh, and that time I stabbed her with a Nutty Royale. And that other time I slammed her hair in my Algebra book.

But, I mean, besides all that.

Anyway, I didn't get a chance to get on my knees and beg her, because the second bell rang, and people started coming into the classroom, including Michael, who came up to me and gave me a bunch of pages he'd printed off the internet about the dangers of dehydration in pregnant women — 'To give to your mom,' he said, kissing me on the cheek (yes, in front of everyone: *Tcha*).

Still, there are shadows over my otherwise exuberant joy: one shadow is, I was unsuccessful in getting my boyfriend's band booked for the prom, thus making it more likely than ever that I will never have my *Pretty in Pink* moment with

Michael. Another shadow is that my best friend is still not speaking to me, nor I to her, because of her psychotic behaviour and mistreatment of her former boyfriend. Yet another shadow is the fact that my first actual published news story ever in the *Atom* reads so incredibly lamely (although they did publish my poem . . . *TRÈS TRÈS TCHA*. Even if I'm the only one who knows it's mine). It isn't exactly my fault my story sucks so much, though. I mean, Lesley hardly gave me enough time to come up with something truly Pulitzer-prize worthy. I'm no Nellie Bly or Ida M. Tarbell, you know. I had a lot of other homework to do too.

Finally, everything is overshadowed by my fear that my mother might pass out again, next time not within sight of Assistant Fire Chief Logan and the rest of Ladder Company Number Three, and of course by my overall dread that, for two whole months this summer, I will be leaving this fair city and everyone in it for the distant shores of Genovia.

Really, if you think about it, this is all entirely too much for one simple fifteen-year-old girl to bear. It is a wonder I have been able to maintain what little composure I have left, under the circumstances.

When adding or subtracting terms that have the same variables, combine the coefficients.

Wednesday, May 7, Gifted and Talented

STRIKE!!!!!!!!!!

They just announced it on TV. Mrs Hill is letting us crowd around the one in the Teachers' Lounge.

I have never been in the Teachers' Lounge before. It is actually not very nice. There are weird stains on the carpet.

But whatever. The point is that the hotel-workers' union has just joined the busboys in their strike. The restaurant union is expected to follow suit shortly. Which means that there will be no one working in the restaurants or the hotels of New York City. The entire metro area could be shut down. The financial loss from tourism and conventions could be in the billions.

And all because of Rommel.

Seriously. Who knew one little hairless dog could cause so much trouble?

To be fair, it is actually not Rommel's fault. It is Grandmère's. I mean, she never should have brought a dog into a restaurant in the first place, even if it IS OK in France. It was weird to see Lilly on TV. I mean, I see Lilly on TV all the time, but this was a major network — well, I mean, it was New York One, which isn't exactly national or anything, but it's watched in more households than Manhattan Public Access, anyway. Not that Lilly was running the press conference. No, it was being run by the heads of the hotel and restaurant unions. But if you looked to the left of the podium, you could see Jangbu standing there, with Lilly at his side, holding a big sign that said LIVING WAGES FOR LIVING BEINGS.

She is so busted. She has an unexcused absence for the day. Principal Gupta will be so calling the Drs Moscovitz tonight.

Michael just shook his head disgustedly at the sight of his sister on a channel other than Fifty-Six. I mean, he is fully on the side of the busboys — they SHOULD be paid a living wage, of course. But Michael is disgusted with Lilly. He says it's because her interest in the welfare of the busboys has more to do with her interest in Jangbu than in the plight of immigrants to this country.

I kind of wish Michael hadn't said anything, though, because you know Boris was sitting right there next to the TV. He looks so pathetic with his head all bandaged and everything. He kept lifting up his hand when he thought no one was looking, and softly tracing Lilly's features on the screen. It was truly touching, to tell you the truth. I actually got tears in my eyes for a minute.

Although they went away when I realized that the TV in the Teachers' Lounge is forty inches, whereas all the TVs in the student media room are only twenty-seven.

Wednesday, May 7, the Plaza

This is unbelievable. I mean, truly. When I walked into the hotel lobby today, all ready for my princess lesson with Grandmère, I was completely unprepared for the chaos that met me at the door. The place is a zoo.

The doorman with the gold epaulettes who usually holds the limo door open for me? Gone.

The bellboys who so efficiently pile up everybody's luggage on to those brass carts? Gone.

The polite concierge at the reception desk? Gone.

And don't even ask about the line for high tea at the Palm Court. It was out of control.

Because of course there was no hostess to seat anybody, or waiters to take anybody's orders.

It was amazing. Lars and I practically had to fight off this family of twelve from like Iowa or whatever who were trying to crowd on to our elevator with the lifesize gorilla they'd just bought at FAO Schwartz across the street. The dad kept yelling, 'There's room! There's room! Come on, kids, squeeze.'

Finally Lars was forced to show the dad his sidearm and go, 'There's no room. Take the next elevator, please,' before the guy backed off, looking pale.

This never would have happened if the elevator attendant had been there. But this afternoon the porters' union declared a sympathy strike, and joined the restaurant and hotel workers in walking off the job.

You would think after everything we'd gone through just to get to my princess lesson on time, Grandmère would have had some sympathy for us when we walked through the door. But instead she was just standing in the middle of the suite, squawking into the phone.

'What do you mean, the kitchen is closed?' she was demanding. 'How can the kitchen be closed? I ordered lunch hours ago, and still haven't received it. I am not hanging up until I speak to the person in charge of Room Service. He knows who I am.'

My dad was sitting on the couch across from Grandmère's TV, watching — what else? — New York One with a tense expression on his face. I sat down beside him, and he looked at me, as if surprised to see me there.

'Oh, Mia,' he said. 'Hello. How is your mother?'

'Fine,' I said, because, even though I hadn't seen her since breakfast I knew she had to be OK, since I hadn't got any calls on my mobile phone. 'She's alternating between Gatorade and PediaLyte. She likes the grape kind. What's happening with the strike?' My dad just shook his head in a defeated way. 'The union representatives are meeting with the Mayor's office. They're hoping to work out a negotiation soon.'

I sighed. 'You realize, of course, that none of this would have happened if I had never been born. Because then I wouldn't have had a birthday dinner.'

My dad looked at me kind of sharply, and went, 'I hope you're not blaming yourself for this, Mia.'

I almost went, 'Are you kidding? I blame Grandmère.' But then I realized from the earnest expression on my dad's face that I had like this huge sympathy quotient going for me, and so instead I went, in this doleful voice, 'It's just too bad I'm going to be in Genovia for most of the summer. It might have been nice if I could have, you know, spent the summer volunteering with an organization seeking to help those unfortunate busboys . . .'

My dad so didn't fall for it, though. He just winked at me and said, 'Nice try.'

Geez! Between him wanting to whisk me off to Genovia for July and August, and my mother offering to take me to her gynaecologist, I am getting way mixed messages from my parental units. It's a wonder I haven't developed a multiple personality. Or Asperger's syndrome. If I don't already have it.

While I was sitting there sulking over my failure to keep from having to spend my precious summer months on the freaking Côte d'Azur, Grandmère started signalling me from the phone. She kept snapping her fingers at me, then pointing at the door to her bedroom. I just sat there blinking at her until finally she put her hand over the receiver and hissed, 'Amelia! In my bedroom! Something for you!'

A present? For *me*? I couldn't imagine what Grandmère could have got me — I mean, the orphan was enough of a gift for one birthday. But I wasn't about to say no to a present . . . at least, not so long as it didn't involve the hide of some slaughtered mammal.

So I got up and went to the door to Grandmère's bedroom, just as someone must have taken Grandmère off hold, since as I turned the knob she was hollering, 'But I ordered that cob salad FOUR HOURS AGO. Do I need to come down there to make it myself ? What do you mean, that would be a public health violation? What public? I want to make a salad for *myself*, not the public!'

I opened the door to Grandmère's room. It is, being the bedroom of the penthouse suite of the Plaza Hotel, a very fancy room, with lots of gold leaf all over everything, and freshly cut flowers all over the place . . . although with the strike, I doubted Grandmère'd be getting new floral arrangements any time soon.

Anyway, as I stood there, looking around the room for my present, and totally saying this little prayer — *Please don't let*

it be a mink stole. Please don't let it be a mink stole — my gaze fell upon this dress that was lying across the bed. It was the colour of Jennifer Lopez's engagement ring from Ben Affleck — the softest pink imaginable — and was covered all over in sparkling pink beading. It was off the shoulder with a sweetheart neckline and this huge, filmy skirt.

I knew right away what it was. And even though it wasn't black or slit up the side, it was still the most beautiful prom dress I had ever seen. It was prettier than the one Rachael Leigh Cook wore in *She's All That*. It was prettier than the one Drew Barrymore wore in *Never Been Kissed*. And it was way, way prettier than the gunnysack Molly Ringwald wore in *Pretty in Pink*. It was even prettier than the prom dress Annie Potts gave Molly Ringwald to wear in *Pretty in Pink*, before Molly went mental with the pinking shears and screwed the whole thing up.

It was the prettiest prom dress I had ever seen.

And as I stood there gazing at it, a huge lump rose in my throat. Because, of course, I wasn't going to the prom.

So I shut the door and turned round and went back to sit on the couch next to my dad, who was still staring, transfixed, at the television screen.

A second later, Grandmère hung up the phone, turned to me, and said, 'Well?'

'It's really beautiful, Grandmère,' I said sincerely.

'I know it's beautiful,' she said. 'Aren't you going to try it on?'

I had to swallow hard in order to talk in anything that sounded like my normal voice.

'I can't,' I said. 'I told you, I'm not going to the prom, Grandmère.'

'Nonsense,' Grandmère said. 'The Sultan called to cancel our dinner tonight — Le Cirque is closed — but this silly strike will be over by Saturday. And then you can go to your little prom.'

'No,' I said. 'It's not because of the strike. It's because of what I told you. You know. About Michael.'

'What about Michael?' my dad wanted to know. Only I really don't like saying anything negative about Michael in front of my father, because he is always just looking for an excuse to hate him, since he is a dad and it is a dad's job to hate his daughter's boyfriend. So far my dad and Michael have managed to get along, and I want to keep it that way.

'Oh,' I said lightly. 'You know. Boys don't really get into the prom the way girls do.'

My dad just grunted and turned back to the TV. 'You can say that again,' he said. He's one to talk! He went to an all-boys high school! He didn't even HAVE a prom!

'Just try it on,' Grandmère said. 'So I can send it back if it needs fitting.'

'Grandmère,' I said. 'There's no point . . .'

But my voice trailed off because Grandmère got That Look in her eye. You know the one. The look that, if Grandmère were a trained assassin and not a dowager princess, would mean somebody is about to get iced.

So I got up off the couch and went back into Grandmère's room and tried on the dress. Of course it fitted perfectly, because Chanel has all my measurements from the last dress Grandmère bought there for me, and God forbid I should grow or anything, particularly in the chest area.

As I stood there gazing at my reflection in the floor-length mirror, I couldn't help thinking how convenient the off-the-shoulder thing is. You know, in the event Michael and I ever wanted to get to second base.

But then I remembered we aren't actually going anywhere together where I would actually get to wear this dress, since Michael had put the whole kibosh on the prom, so it was kind of a moot point. Sadly, I peeled off the dress and put it back on Grandmère's bed. Probably there'll be some function I'll end up wearing it to in Genovia this summer. Some function Michael won't even be there to attend. Which is just so typical.

I came out of the bedroom just in time to see Lilly on TV. She was addressing a room full of reporters at what looked like the Chinatown Holiday Inn again. She was going, 'I would just like to say that none of this would be happening if the Dowager Princess of Genovia would publicly admit her culpability in her failure to control her dog, and in bringing said dog into a dining establishment.'

Grandmère's jaw dropped. My dad just kept staring stonily into the TV.

'As proof of this claim,' Lilly said, holding up a copy of today's edition of the *Atom*, 'I offer this editorial written by the Dowager Princess's own granddaughter.'

And then I listened in horror as Lilly, in a sing-song voice, read my article out loud. And I must say, hearing my own words thrown back at me in that manner really made me cognizant of just how stupid they sounded . . . far more so than, say, hearing them read in my own voice.

Oops. Dad and Grandmère are staring at me. They do not look happy. In fact, they look kind of . . .

Wednesday, May 7, 10 p.m., the Loft

I really don't get why they're so upset. It is a journalist's duty to report the truth, and that is what I did. If they can't take the heat, they both need to get out of the kitchen. I mean, Grandmère DID take her dog into that restaurant, and Jangbu DID only trip because Rommel darted out in front of him. They cannot deny this. They can wish it hadn't happened and they can wish that Lesley Cho had not asked me to write an editorial about it.

But they cannot deny it, and they cannot blame me for exercising my journalistic rights. Not to mention my journalistic integrity.

Now I know how the great reporters before me must have felt. Ernie Pyle, for his hard-hitting reportage during World War II. Ethel Payne, first lady of the black press during the civil rights movement. Margaret Higgins, the first woman to win a Pulitzer for international reporting. Lois Lane, for her tireless efforts on behalf of the *Daily Planet*. Those Woodward and Bernstein guys, for the whole Watergate thing, whatever that was about.

I know now exactly what it must have been like for them. The pressure. The threats of grounding. The phone calls to their mothers.

That's the part that hurt the most, really. That they would bother my poor dehydrated mother, who is busy trying to bring a *new life* into the world. God knows her kidneys are probably rattling around in her body like packs of desiccant right now. And they dare to pester her with such trivialities?

Plus, my mom is so on my side. I don't know what Dad was thinking. Did he really think Mom would be on Grandmère's side in all this?

Although Mom did tell me that to keep peace in the family I should at least apologize. I don't see why I should, though. This whole thing has resulted in nothing but heartache for me. Not only did it cause the break-up of one of AEHS's most long-term couples, but it caused me to have what looks to be a permanent falling-out with my best friend. I have lost MY BEST FRIEND over this.

I informed both Dad and Grandmère of this right before the latter imperiously ordered Lars to get me out of her sight. Fortunately, I had the foresight to snag the prom dress out of Grandmère's room and stuff it in my backpack before this happened. It's only a little wrinkled. A good steaming in the shower and it will be good as new.

I can't help thinking that they could have handled this little affair in a more appropriate manner. They COULD have called a press conference of their own, fessed up to the whole dog-in-the-restaurant thing, and had it all over and done with.

But no. And now it's too late. Even if Grandmère fesses up, it's highly unlikely the hotel, restaurant and porters' unions are going to back down NOW.

Well, I guess it's just another case of people failing to pay heed to the voice of youth. And now they're just going to have to suffer.

Too bad.

Thursday, May 8, Homeroom

OH MY GOD!!!!!!!!!!!!!!!! THEY'VE CANCELLED THE PROM!!!!!!!!!!!!!!!!!!

The Atom

The Official Student-Run Newspaper of Albert Einstein High School

PROM CANCELLED!!!!!!!!

By Lesley Cho

Due to the city-wide hotel, restaurant and porters' unions strike, this year's Senior Prom has been cancelled. The restaurant Maxim's notified school officials that due to the strike they would be closing, effective immediately. The Prom Committee's $4,000 deposit was returned. This year's senior class is left high and dry with no alternative but to have the prom in the school cafeteria, something Prom Committee members considered, but then dismissed.

'The prom is special,' said Prom Committee chairperson, Lana Weinberger. 'It's no ordinary school dance. We can't just have it in the cafeteria, as if it were another Cultural Diversity or Non-Denominational Winter Dance. We'd rather have no prom than a prom where we're stepping on old French fries or whatever.'

Not everyone in the school agrees with the Prom Committee's controversial decision, however. Said senior Judith Gershner, when she heard of Lana Weinberger's remarks, 'We've been looking forward to our prom since we were ninth graders. To have it taken away now, over something as trivial as stray French fries, seems a bit petty. I would rather have French fries stuck to my heel at the prom than no prom at all.'

The Prom Committee remains adamant, however, that it will have the prom off school grounds, or not at all.

'There's nothing special about coming to school dressed up,' ninth grader Lana Weinberger commented. 'If we're going to get dressed up to the nines, we want to be going somewhere other than where we have gone every morning all year long.'

The cause of the strike, which was summarized in this week's edition of the *Atom*, still appears to have been an incident which occurred at the restaurant Les Hautes Manger, where AEHS freshman and Genovian Princess Mia Thermopolis dined last week with her grandmother. Says Lilly Moscovitz, former friend of the princess and chairperson of the Students Against the Wrongful Dismissal of Jangbu Pinasa Association, 'It's all Mia's fault. Or at least her grandmother's. All we want is Jangbu's job back, and a formal apology from Clarisse Renaldo. Oh, and vacation and sick pay, as well as health benefits, for busboys city-wide.'

Princess Mia was, at the time of going to press, unavailable for comment, being, according to her mother, Helen Thermopolis, in the shower.

We here at the *Atom* will attempt to keep all of you informed as strike negotiations progress.

Oh my God. THANKS, MOM. THANKS FOR TELLING ME THE SCHOOL PAPER CALLED WHILE I WAS IN THE SHOWER.

You should SEE the dirty looks I got as I made my way to my locker this morning. Thank God I have an armed bodyguard, or I might have been in some serious trouble. Some of those girls on the Varsity Lacrosse team – the ones who smoke and do chin-ups in the third floor girls' room – made EXTREMELY threatening hand gestures towards me as I got out of the limo. Someone had even written on Joe the stone lion (in chalk, but still) GENOVIA SUCKS.

GENOVIA SUCKS!!!!!!!!! The reputation of my principality

is being besmirched, and all because of a stupid dance being cancelled!

Oh, all right. I know the prom is not stupid. I mean, I, of all people, KNOW that the prom is not stupid. It is a vitally important part of the high-school experience, as Molly Ringwald can all too readily attest!

And yet, because of me, it is being ripped from the hearts and yearbooks of the members of this year's AEHS graduating class. I've GOT to do something. Only what???? WHAT????????????

Thursday, May 8. Algebra

You will never believe what Lana just said to me. I completely kid you not.

Lana: (swivelling round in her chair and glaring at me) You did this on purpose, didn't you? Caused this strike and made the prom get cancelled.

Me: What? No. What are you talking about?

Lana: Just admit it. You did it because I wouldn't let your boyfriend's stupid band stink up the place. Admit it.

Me: No! That's not it at all. It wasn't me, anyway. It was my grandmother.

Lana: Whatever. All you Genovians are the same.

Then she whipped back round, before I could say another word.

All you Genovians? Um, excuse me, but I'm the only Genovian Lana has ever even met.

She has some nerve . . .

Thursday. May 8. Bio

Mia, are you all right?

> Yes, Shameeka. It was just an apple core.

Still. That was way cool how Lars hit that guy. Your bodyguard has some sharp reflexes there.

> Yeah, well. That's why he got the job. So how come you're speaking to me? Don't you hate me too? I mean, after all, you and Jeff were going to go to the prom.

Well, it's not YOUR fault it got cancelled. Besides, I wouldn't have had that much fun at it anyway. I mean, not if the only other girl from my class was going to be LANA!!!!!!!!!!
By the way, did you hear about Tina?

> No. What?

Yesterday, when Boris was waiting at his locker for Lilly - you know, he put that Happy Ad in the paper, asking her to meet him there after school, so they could talk?

235

Well, Tina decided to meet him, you know, and ask him if he wanted to grab a frozen hot chocolate at Serendipity, because she felt so sorry for him and all. Well, I guess he finally gave up on waiting for Lilly, since he said yes and the two of them went, and this morning, I swear I saw them holding hands beside the foamcore sculpture of the Parthenon outside the language lab.

> WAIT A MINUTE. WHAT? YOU SAW TINA AND BORIS HOLDING HANDS. TINA AND BORIS. TINA and *BORIS PELKOWSKI*????

Yes.

> Tina. Tina Hakim Baba. And Boris Pelkowski. TINA AND BORIS?????????

YES!!!!!!!!!!

Oh my God. What is happening to the world we live in?

236

Thursday, May 8, third-floor stairwell

Shameeka and I cornered Tina after we came out of Bio, and dragged her up here to demand confirmation of the holding-hands-with-Boris thing. I am skipping Health and Safety, but who cares? I would only end up sitting there under the hostile gazes of my fellow Health and Safety practitioners, one of whom includes my ex-best friend Lilly Moscovitz, whom I have absolutely no desire to speak to anyway.

Besides, my Asperger's syndrome report is due, and I didn't exactly have a chance to finish it, due to the severe emotional problems I am suffering right now on account of my mother's bladder problems and my boyfriend's refusal to take me to the prom and the whole strike thing and all.

I cannot believe the stuff that is spilling out of Tina's mouth. About how, all her life, she's just been looking for a man who could love her the way heroes in the romance novels she likes to read so much love their heroines. About how she never thought she would meet a man who could love a woman with the intensity of the heroes she admires most, like Mr Rochester and Heathcliff and Colonel Brandon and Mr Darcy and Spider-Man and all.

Then she says that watching the way Boris fell apart after Lilly left him for Jangbu Pinasa made her realize that out of all the boys she had ever met he was the only one who seemed close to fitting her description of the perfect boyfriend. Except, of course, for the whole looks thing. But, other than that, he is everything Tina has ever wanted in a boyfriend:

- **Loyal**
  (Well, that goes without saying. Boris would never even LOOK at another girl after he hooked up with Lilly.)
- **Passionate**
  (Uh, I guess the whole globe thing proved Boris is deeply passionate. Or suffers from Asperger's syndrome.)
- **Intelligent**
  (4.0 GPA.)
- **Musical**
  (As I can only too readily testify.)
- **In touch with popular culture**
  (He does watch *Buffy*.)
- **Fond of Chinese food**
  (This is true as well.)
- **Absolutely uninterested in competitive sports**
  (Except figure skating. Well, he *is* Russian.)

Plus, Tina adds, he is a really good kisser, once he takes out his bionater.

A REALLY GOOD KISSER, ONCE HE TAKES OUT HIS BIONATER.

You know what that means, don't you? IT MEANS THAT TINA AND BORIS HAVE KISSED! How would she know this if they hadn't????????

Oh my God. I can't stop gagging. I like Boris — I really do. I mean, except for the fact that he is COMPLETELY INSANE I think he is a really nice guy. He is sensitive and funny and, if you can forget the asthma inhaler and the mouth-breathing and the violin playing and the whole sweater thing, yeah, OK I guess he is PASSABLY attractive.

I mean, at least he is taller than Tina.

BUT OH MY GOD!!!!!!!!!!!! BORIS PELKOWSKI, TINA'S MR ROCHESTER?????

NO, NO, NO, A THOUSAND TIMES NO!!!!!!!!!!!!!!!!!!!!!!!

But as Shameeka just pointed out to me (while Tina was checking her text messages), Boris doesn't necessarily have to be her Mr Rochester for all eternity. He could just be her Mr Rochester for, you know, now. Until her real Mr Rochester comes along.

Oh my God. I just don't know. I mean, BORIS PELKOWSKI.

Well, at least Tina's right about one thing: he does feel

things passionately. I have the blood-soaked sweater to prove it. Well, not really, because Mrs Pelkowski returned it and the dry cleaner really did get out all the stains.

But still.

Tina and BORIS PELKOWSKI?????????????

AAAAAAAAAAAAAAAAAAAAAHHHHHHHHHHHH!!!!!!!!!!

!!

Thursday, May 8, the Loft

After Lars had to shield me from yet another projectile — this one thrown with stunning accuracy by a senior rugby player — he called my dad and said he thought for safety reasons I should be removed from school premises.

So my dad said OK. So I get the rest of the day off.

Except not really, because Mr G is going over everything I haven't been paying much attention to in his class for the past week and a half, using the front of the refrigerator as a chalk board, and the magnetic alphabet as the coefficients in the problems I'm supposed to be solving.

Whatever, Mr G. Can't you see I have way bigger problems right now than a sinking grade in your class? I mean, hello, I cannot even set foot in my own school without being pelted with fruit.

I'm so depressed. I mean, after everything with the strike, and then with Tina, and now this thing with everybody hating me, I really don't see how I'm going to make it through the rest of the week. I already called my dad and was like, 'Tell Grandmère thanks a lot. Now I'm not even safe at my own institution of secondary education, and it's all her fault.'

I don't know if he told her, though. I'm not sure he and Grandmère are speaking any more.

I know I'M not speaking to Grandmère. It seems like I'm not speaking to a lot of people, actually . . . Grandmère, Lilly, Lana Weinberger . . .

Well, I've never really been on speaking terms with Lana. But you know what I mean. Wow, what if I can never go back to school again? Like, what if I have to be home-schooled? That would suck so bad! I mean, how would I keep up with all the gossip? Like who was going out with whom? And when would I ever see Michael? Just on weekends, and that's it. That would be so WRONG!!!! The high point of my day is seeing him waiting outside his building to be picked up by my limo on the way to school. I know that I am going to be deprived of this forever when he starts going to Columbia. But I thought I'd still be able to enjoy it for the rest of the school year, anyway.

Oh my God, this is bumming me out so badly. I mean, I never really LIKED Albert Einstein High, but considering the alternatives . . . you know, home-schooling or, even worse, school in GENOVIA . . . My God, in comparison, AEHS is like Shangri-La. Whatever Shangri-La is.

How dare they try to keep me from it? AEHS, I mean. HOW DARE THEY?????????? Oh, someone is at the door. Please let it be Michael with the rest of my homework. Not because I'm desperate to do the rest of my homework, but because if I have ever needed to be comforted with the smell of Michael's neck, it's now . . .

PLEASE PLEASE PLEASE PLEASE PLEASE PLEASE PLEASE PLEASE.

Thursday, May 8, later, the Loft

Well, it wasn't Michael. But it was close. It was a Moscovitz.

Just the wrong one.

I really think Lilly has some nerve coming round here after what she put me through. I mean, Asperger's or not, she has made my life a perfect hell these past few days, and then she shows up at my door, crying and begging to be forgiven?

But what could I do? I couldn't exactly slam the door in her face. Well, I could have, of course, but it would have been terribly unprincesslike.

Instead, I invited her in — but coldly. *Very* coldly. Who's the weak one NOW, I'd like to know????

We went into my room. I shut the door (I'm allowed to shut my bedroom door so long as anybody but Michael is inside there with me).

And Lilly let loose.

Not, as I was expecting, with the heartfelt apology I deserved for her dreadful treatment of me, dragging my good name and royal lineage across the airwaves in the manner she had.

Oh no. Nothing like that. Instead, Lilly is crying because she heard about Tina and Boris.

244

That's right. Lilly's crying because she wants her boyfriend back.

Seriously! And after the way she'd treated him!

I'm just sitting here in stunned silence, staring at Lilly as she rants. She's stomping around my room in her Mao jacket and Birkenstocks, shaking her glossy curls, her eyes, behind the lenses of her glasses (I guess revolutionaries working to empower the people don't wear their contacts), filled with bitter tears.

'How could he?' she keeps wailing. 'I turn my back for five minutes — five minutes! — and he runs off with another girl? What can he be thinking?'

I can't help but point out that perhaps Boris was thinking about seeing her, Lilly, his girlfriend, with another boy's tongue down her throat. In MY hallway closet, no less.

'Boris and I never vowed to see one another exclusively,' she insists. 'I told him that I am like a restless bird . . . I can't be tied down.'

'Well.' I shrug. 'Maybe he's more into the roosting type.'

'Like Tina, you mean?' Lilly rubs her eyes. 'I can't believe she could do this to me. I mean, doesn't she realize that she'll never make Boris happy? He's a genius, after all. It takes a genius to know how to handle a fellow genius.'

I remind Lilly, somewhat stiffly, that *I* am no genius, but

245

I seem to be handling her brother, whose IQ is 179, quite well.

I don't mention the whole part about him still refusing to go to the prom and the fact that we haven't got to second base yet.

'Oh, please,' Lilly scoffs. 'Michael's gaga for you. Besides, at least you're in Gifted and Talented. You get to observe geniuses in action on a daily basis. What does Tina know about them? Why, I don't think she's even seen *A Beautiful Mind*! Because Russell doesn't take his shirt off enough in it, no doubt.'

'Hey,' I say harshly. I'd noticed this about *A Beautiful Mind* too, and I think it's a valid criticism. 'Tina is my friend. A way better friend to me than *you've* been lately.'

Lilly has the grace to look guilty.

'I'm sorry about all that, Mia,' she says. 'I swear I don't know what came over me. I just saw Jangbu and I . . . well, I guess I became a slave to my own lust.'

I must say, I am very surprised to hear this. Because while Jangbu is, of course, quite hot, I never knew physical attraction was important to Lilly. I mean, after all, she's been going out with Boris for, like, ever.

But apparently it was all completely physical between her and Jangbu.

God. I wonder what base they got to. Would it be rude

to ask? I mean, I know that, considering we aren't best friends any more, it probably isn't any of my business. But if she got to third with that guy, I'll kill her.

'But it's over between Jangbu and me,' Lilly just announced very dramatically . . . so dramatically that Fat Louie, who doesn't like Lilly very much in the first place, and usually hides in the closet among my shoes when she comes over, just tried to burrow his way into my snow boots. 'I thought he had the heart of a proletarian. I thought at last I had found a man who shared my passion for social causes and the advancement of the worker. But alas . . . I was wrong. So very, very wrong. I simply cannot be soulmates with a man willing to sell his life story to the press.'

It appears that Jangbu has been approached by a number of magazines, including *People* and *US Weekly*, who are vying for the exclusive rights to the details of his run-in with the Dowager Princess of Genovia and her dog.

'Really?' I was very surprised to hear this. 'How much are they offering him?'

'Last time I talked to him, they were up to six figures.' Lilly dries her eyes on one of Grandmère's Chanel scarves. 'He won't be needing his job back at Les Hautes Manger, that's for sure. He's planning on opening a restaurant of his own. A Taste of Tibet, he's planning on calling it.'

'Wow.' I feel for Lilly. I really do. I mean, I know how much it sucks when someone you thought was your spiritual lifemate turns out to be sell-out. Especially when he French kisses as well as Josh — I mean Jangbu — does.

Still, just because I feel sorry for Lilly doesn't mean I'm going to forgive her for what she did. I may not be self-actualized, but at least I have pride.

'But I want you to know,' Lilly is saying, 'that I realized I wasn't in love with Jangbu before all this stuff with the strike happened. I knew I had never stopped loving Boris when he picked up that globe and dropped it on his head for me. I mean, Mia, he was willing to get *stitches* for me. That's how much he loves me. No boy has ever loved me enough to risk actual, physical pain and discomfort for me . . . and certainly not Jangbu. I mean, he's WAY too caught up in his own fame and celebrity. Not like Boris. I mean, Boris is a thousand times more gifted and talented than Jangbu, and HE isn't caught up in the fame game.'

I really don't know quite how to respond to all this. I guess Lilly must realize this by the way she's narrowing her eyes at me and going, 'Would you please stop writing in that journal for ONE MINUTE and tell me how I can win Boris back?'

Though it pained me to do it, I was forced to inform Lilly that I think the chances of her ever winning Boris back are like zero. Less than zero, even. Like in the negative polynomials.

'Tina is really crazy about him,' I told her. 'And I think he feels the same way about her. I mean, he gave her his autographed eight-by-ten glossy of Joshua Bell—'

This information caused Lilly to clutch her heart in existential pain. Or maybe not so existential, since I'm not even really sure what existential means. In any case, she clutched her heart and fell back dramatically across my bed.

'That witch!' she keeps yelling — so loudly that I'm afraid any minute Mr G is going to come busting in here, thinking we have *Buffy* turned up too loud. Also, she wasn't actually saying witch, but the other word that rhymes with it. 'That black-hearted, back-stabbing witch! I'll get her for stealing my man! I'll get her!'

I had to get very severe with Lilly. I told her that under no circumstances was she going to 'get' anyone. I told her that Tina really and sincerely adored Boris, which is all he has ever wanted — to love and be loved in return, just like Ewan McGregor in *Moulin Rouge*. I told her that if she really loved Boris the way she said she did, she would leave him and Tina alone, let them enjoy the last few weeks of school together. Then if, in the autumn, Lilly still found herself wanting Boris back, she could say something. But not before.

Lilly was, I think, a little taken aback by my sage —

and very direct — advice. In fact, she still appears to be digesting it. She's sitting on the end of my bed, blinking at my Princess Leia screensaver. I am sure it must be quite a blow to a girl with an ego the size of Lilly's . . . you know, that a boy who had once loved her could learn to love again. But she will just have to get used to it. Because after what she put Boris through this week I for one will see to it that she never, ever dates him again. If I have to stand in front of Boris with a big old sword, like Aragorn in front of that Frodo dude, I will totally do it. That is how determined I am that Lilly will never again mess with Boris Pelkowski's heavily bandaged, misshapen genius head.

I don't know if she could see how fiercely I was writing that, or if there was something particularly determined in my expression, or what. But Lilly just sighed and went, 'Oh, all *right*.'

Now she is putting on her coat and leaving. Because even though she and Jangbu have parted ways, she is still chair person of SATWDOJPA and has loads to do.

None of which apparently includes apologizing to me.

Or so I thought.

At my door, Lilly turned and said, 'Listen, Mia. I'm sorry I called you weak the other day. You're not weak. In fact . . . you're one of the strongest people I know.'

Hello! So true! I have battled so many demons in my day,

I make those girls on *Charmed* look like the ones on freaking *Full House*. Really, I should get a medal, or at least the key to the city, or something.

Sadly, however, just when I thought my bravery was no longer going to be needed — Lilly and I had hugged, and she'd left, after a few words of apology to my mom and Mr G over the whole making-out-in-our-hall-closet-with Jangbu-the-unemployed-busboy thing, which they'd graciously accepted — the buzzer in the vestibule went off AGAIN. I thought for SURE it had to be Michael this time. He'd promised to collect and bring over all my remaining assignments.

So you can imagine my horror — my absolute revulsion — when I bounded over to the intercom, hit the Talk button, went, 'Hellooo-ooooo?' and the voice that came crackling over it in response was not the deep, warm, familiar voice of my one true love . . . but the hideous cackle of Grandmère!!!!!!!!!!!!!!

Thursday, May 8, 1 a.m., the futon couch in the Loft

This is a nightmare. It has to be. Somebody is going to pinch me and I'm going to wake up and it's all going to be over and I'm going to be back snug in my own bed, not out here on this futon — how come I never noticed how HARD this thing is? — in the living room in the middle of the night.

Except that it's NOT a nightmare. I know it's not a nightmare, because to have a nightmare you actually have to fall ASLEEP, something I can't do, because Grandmère is SNORING TOO LOUDLY.

That's right. My grandmother snores. Some scoop for the *Post*, huh? I should give them a call and hold up the phone to the door to my room (you can hear her even with the door CLOSED). I can just see the headline:

DOWAGER PRINCESS
SNORES LIKE A
JACKHAMMER

I can't believe this is happening. Like my life isn't bad enough. Like I don't have enough problems now my psychotic grandmother has *moved in* with me. I could hardly believe it when I opened the Loft door and saw her standing there, her driver right behind her with about fifty million Louis Vuitton bags. I just stared at her for a full minute, until finally Grandmère went, 'Well, Amelia? Aren't you going to ask me in?'

And then, before I even had a chance to, she just barged right by me, complaining the whole way about how we don't have an elevator and did we have any idea what a walk up three flights of stairs could do to a woman her age (I noticed that she didn't mention what it could do to a chauffeur who had been forced to carry all her luggage up the same aforementioned three flights of stairs)?

Then she started walking around the Loft like she always does when she comes over, picking up things and looking at them with a disapproving expression on her face before putting them down again, like Mom's Cinco de Mayo skeleton collection, and Mr G's NCAA Final Four drink holders.

Meanwhile, my mom and Mr G, having heard all the commotion, came out of their room and then froze — both of them — in horror as they took in the sight before them. I have to admit, it did look a bit scary . . . especially since by then Rommel had worked his way free from Grandmère's bag and was staggering around the floor on his spindly Bambi legs, sniffing things so carefully you would have thought he expected them to explode in his face at any given moment (which, when he gets around to sniffing Fat Louie, might actually happen).

'Um, Clarisse,' my mother (brave woman!) said. 'Would you mind telling us what you're doing here? With, er, what appears to be your entire wardrobe in tow?'

'I cannot stay at that hotel a moment longer,' Grandmère said, putting down Mr G's lava lamp and not even glancing at my mother, whose pregnancy — 'At her advanced age,' Grandmère likes to say, even though Mom is actually younger than many recently pregnant starlets — she considers an embarrassment of grand proportions. 'No one works there any more! The place is completely chaotic. You cannot get a soul to bring up a morsel of Room Service, and forget about getting someone to run your bath. And so I've come here.' She blinked at us less than fondly. 'To the bosom of my family. In times of need, I believe it is traditional for relatives to take one another in.'

My mom totally wasn't falling for Grandmère's poor-little-me act.

'Clarisse,' she said, folding her arms over her chest (which is quite a feat, considering how big her boobs have got — I can only hope that if I ever get pregnant my own knockers will swell to such heroic proportions). 'There is a hotel workers' strike. No one is exactly lobbing SCUD missiles at the Plaza. I think you've lost your perspective a little bit . . .'

Just then the phone rang. I, of course, thinking it was Michael, dived for it. But, alas, it was not Michael. It was my father.

'Mia,' he said, sounding a trifle panicked. 'Is your grandmother there?'

'Why, yes, Dad,' I said. 'She is. Would you care to speak with her?'

'Oh, God,' my dad groaned. 'No. Let me talk to your mother.'

My dad was totally in for it, and did he ever know it. I handed the phone to my mom, who took it with the expression of long-suffering she always wears in Grandmère's presence. Just as she was putting the phone to her ear, Grandmère said to her chauffeur, 'That will be all, Gaston. You can put the bags down in Amelia's room, then leave.'

'Stay where you are, Gaston,' my mom said, just as I yelled, 'MY room? Why MY room?'

Grandmère looked at me all acidly and went, 'Because in times of hardship, young lady, it is traditional for the youngest member of the family to sacrifice her comfort for the oldest.'

I have never heard of this cockamamie tradition before.

What was it, like the ten-course Genovian wedding supper, or something?

'Phillipe,' my mom was growling into the phone. 'What is going on here?'

Meanwhile, Mr G was trying to make the best out of a bad situation. He asked Grandmère if he could get her some form of refreshment.

'Sidecar, please,' Grandmère said, not even looking at him, but at the magnetic alphabet Algebra problems on the refrigerator door. 'Easy on the ice.'

'Phillipe!' my mother was saying, in tones of mounting urgency, into the phone.

But it didn't do any good. There was nothing my father could do. He and the staff — Lars, Hans, Gaston, et al. — were OK to rough it at the Plaza under the new, Room-Service free conditions. But Grandmère just couldn't take it. She had apparently tried to ring for her nightly chamomile tea and biscotti, and when she'd found out there was no one to bring it to her she'd gone completely mental and stuck her foot through the glass mail chute (endangering the poor postman's fingers when he comes to collect the mail at the bottom of the chute tomorrow).

'But, Phillipe,' my mom kept wailing. 'Why *here*?'

But there was nowhere else for Grandmère to go. Things were just as bad, if not worse, at all the other hotels in the city. Grandmère had finally decided to pack up and abandon ship . . . figuring, no doubt, that as she had a granddaughter fifty blocks away, why not take advantage of the free labour?

So for the moment, anyway, we're stuck with her. I even had to give her my bed, because she categorically refused to sleep on the futon couch. She and Rommel are in *my* room — my safe haven, my sanctuary, my fortress of solitude, my meditation chamber, my Zen palace — where she already unplugged my computer because she didn't like my Princess Leia screensaver 'staring' at her. Poor Fat Louie is so confused he actually hissed at the toilet, because he had to express his disapproval of the whole situation somehow. Now he has hidden himself away in the hall closet — the same closet where, if you think about it, all of this started — amid the vacuum-cleaner parts and all the three-dollar umbrellas we've left there over the years.

It was an extremely frightening sight when Grandmère came out of my bathroom with her hair all in curlers and her night cream on. She looked like something out of the Jedi Council scene in *Attack of the Clones*. I was about to ask her where she'd parked her landspeeder. Except that Mom told me I have to be nice to her — 'At least until I can think of some way to get rid of her, Mia.'

Thank God Michael finally did show up with my home-work. We could not exchange tender greetings, however, because Grandmère was sitting at the kitchen table, watching us like a hawk the whole time. I never even got to smell his neck!

And now I am lying here on this lumpy futon, listening to my grandmother's deep, rhythmic snoring from the other room, and all I can think is that this strike better be over soon.

Because it is bad enough living with a neurotic cat, a drum-playing Algebra teacher, and a woman in her last trimester of pregnancy. Throw in a dowager princess of Genovia, and I'm sorry: book me a room on the twenty-first floor of Bellevue, because it's the funny farm for me.

Friday, May 9, Homeroom

I decided to go to school today because:

1. It's Senior Skip Day, so most of the people who'd like to see me dead aren't here to throw things at me, and
2. It's better than staying at home.

I mean it. It is bad in Apt. 4, 1111 Thompson Street. This morning when Grandmère woke up the first thing she did was demand that I bring her some hot water with lemon and honey in a glass. I was like, 'Um, no way,' which did not go over real well, let me tell you. I thought Grandmère was going to hit me.

Instead, she threw my Fiesta Giles action figure — the one of Buffy the Vampire Slayer's watcher, Giles, in a sombrero — against the wall! I tried to explain to her that he is a collector's item and worth nearly twice what I paid for him, but she was fully unappreciative of my lecture. She just went, 'Get me a hot water with lemon and honey or I shall destroy all of your Bippy the Monster Catcher characters!'

God. She can't even get the name of my favourite show right. I'd like to know how she'd feel, if I didn't pay attention next time she starts in about the Genovian bill of rights, or whatever.

So I got her her stinking hot water with lemon and honey, and she drank it down, and then, I kid you not, she spent about half an hour in my bathroom. I have no idea what she was doing in there, but it nearly drove Fat Louie and I insane . . . me because I needed to get in there to get my toothbrush, and Fat Louie because that's where his litter box is.

But, whatever, I finally got in and brushed my teeth, and then I was like, 'See ya,' and Mr G and I fully raced for the door.

Not fast enough, though, because my mom caught us before we could get safely out of the apartment, and hissed at us in this very scary voice, '*I will get you both for leaving me alone with her all day today. I don't know how, and I don't know when. But when you least expect it . . . expect it.*'

Whoa, Mom. Have some more PediaLyte.

Anyway, things here at school have calmed down a lot since yesterday. Maybe because the seniors aren't here. Well, all except for Michael. He's here. Because, he says, he doesn't believe in skipping just because Josh Richter says to. Also because Principal Gupta is giving ten demerits to every student with an unexcused absence for the day, and if you get demerits the school librarian won't give you a discount at the end-of-year used-book sale, and Michael has had his eye on the school's collected works of Isaac Asimov for some time now.

But really I think he's here for the same reason I am: to escape his current home situation. That's because, he told me in the limo on the way up to school, Lilly's parents finally found out about how she's been skipping school and holding press conferences without their permission. The Drs Moscovitz supposedly went full-on Reverend and Mrs Camden and are making Lilly stay home with them today so they can have a nice long talk about her obvious dis-establishmentarianism and the way she treated Boris. Michael was like, 'I was so outta there,' for which who can blame him?

But things are definitely looking up because when we stopped by Ho's this morning before school to buy breakfast (egg sandwich for Michael; Ring Dings for me) he fully grabbed me while Lars was in the refrigerated section buying his morning can of Red Bull and started kissing me, and I got to smell his neck, which instantly soothed my Grandmère-frazzled nerves and convinced me that somehow, some way, everything is going to be all right.

Maybe.

Friday, May 9, Algebra

Oh my God, I can barely write, my hands are shaking so badly. I cannot believe what just happened . . . cannot believe it because it is so GOOD. How is this possible? Good things NEVER happen to me. Well, except for Michael.

But this . . .

It is almost too good to be believed.

What happened was I came into the Algebra classroom all unsuspectingly, not expecting a thing. I sat down in my seat and started taking out last night's homework — which Mr G fully helped me finish — when all of a sudden, my mobile rang.

Thinking my mom was going into labour — or had passed out in the ice-cream section of the Grand Union again — I hurried to answer it.

But it wasn't my mother. It was Grandmère.

'Mia,' she said. 'There's nothing to worry about. I've taken care of the problem.'

I swear I didn't know what she was talking about. Not at first, anyway. I was like, 'What problem?' I thought maybe she was talking about Verl and his noise complaints against us. I thought maybe she'd had him executed, or something.

Well, it's possible, knowing Grandmère.

Which is why her next words were such a total shock.

'Your prom,' she said. 'I spoke to someone. And I've found a place where you can have it, strike or no strike. It's all settled.'

I just sat there for a minute, holding the phone to my ear, barely able to register what I'd just heard.

'Wait,' I said. 'What?'

'For God's sake,' Grandmère said all testily. 'Must I repeat myself? I have found a place for you to have your little prom.'

And then she told me where.

I hung up in a daze. I couldn't believe it. I swear I couldn't believe it.

Grandmère had done it.

Oh, not fessed up to her role in causing one of the most expensive strikes in the history of New York City. Nothing like that.

No. This was more important.

She'd saved the prom. Grandmère had saved the Albert Einstein High School Senior Prom.

I looked at Lana sitting in front of me, resolutely not glancing in my direction, due to the fact that I was the one who'd caused the prom to be cancelled.

And that's when it hit me. Grandmère had saved the prom for AEHS. But I could still save the prom for me.

I poked Lana in the shoulder and went, 'Did you hear?'

Lana turned to stare at me in a very mean way. 'Hear what, freak?'she demanded.

'My grandmother found an alternative space to hold the prom,' I said.

And told her where.

Lana just stared at me in total shock. Really. She was so stunned, she couldn't talk. I'd stunned Lana into silence. Not like that time I'd stabbed her with a Nutty Royale, either.

That time, she'd had a LOT to say.

This time? Nothing.

'But there's just one condition,' I went on.

And then I told her the condition.

Which, of course, Grandmère hadn't brought up. The condition, I mean. No, the condition was a little princess-of-Genovia manoeuvring all of my own.

But hey. I learned from a master.

'So,' I said in conclusion, in an almost friendly way, as if Lana and I were buddies, and not sworn mortal enemies, like Alyssa Milano and the Source of All Evil. 'Take it, or leave it.'

Lana didn't hesitate. Not even a second. She went, 'OK.'

Just like that. 'OK.'

And suddenly, it was like I was Molly Ringwald. I'm not kidding, either.

I cannot explain, not even to myself, why I did what I did next. I just did it. It was like for a moment I was possessed by the spirit of some other girl, a girl who actually gets along with people like Lana. I reached out, grabbed Lana's head, pulled it towards me and gave her a great big kiss, smack in the middle of her eyebrows.

'Ew, gross,' Lana said, backing away fast. 'What is wrong with you, freak?'

But I didn't care that Lana had called me a freak. Twice. Because my heart was singing like those little birds who fly around Snow White's head when she's hanging out by the wishing well. I went, 'Stay right here,' and ran out of my seat . . .

. . . much to the surprise of Mr G, who had just come into the room, his Starbucks Grande in hand.

'Mia,' he said bewilderedly as I darted past him. 'Where are you going? The second bell just rang.'

'Be back in a minute, Mr G,' I called over my shoulder as I raced down the hall to the room where Michael has AP English.

I didn't have to worry about making a fool of myself in front of Michael's peers or anything, since none of Michael's peers were around, it being Senior Skip Day and all. I leaped into his classroom — the first time I had ever done such a thing: usually, of course, Michael visited me in MY classroom — and went, 'Excuse me, Mrs Weinstein,' to his English teacher, 'but may I have a word with Michael?'

Mrs Weinstein — who you could tell had been anticipating a light work day, since she'd come armed with the latest *Cosmo* — looked up from the Bedside Astrologer and went, 'Whatever, Mia.'

So I bounded over to an extremely surprised Michael and, slipping into the desk in front of his, said, 'Michael, remember how you said that you'd only go to the prom if the guys in your band went too?'

Michael couldn't seem to fathom the fact that I was actually in *his* classroom for a change.

'What are you doing here?' he wanted to know. 'Does Mr G know you're here? You're going to get into trouble again . . .'

'Never mind that,' I said. 'Just tell me. Did you mean it when you said you'd go to the prom if the guys from your band went too?'

'I guess so,' Michael said. 'But, Mia, the prom got cancelled, remember?'

'What if I told you,' I said all casually, like I was talking about the weather, 'that the prom was back on, and that they need a band, and that the band the Prom Committee has chosen is YOURS?'

Michael just stared. 'I'd say . . . get out of town.'

'I am totally serious,' I informed him. 'And I will not get out of town. Oh, Michael, *please* say yes, I want to go to the prom *so badly* . . .'

Michael looked surprised. 'You do? But the prom is so . . . lame.'

'I know it's lame,' I said, not without some feeling. 'I know it is, Michael. But that does not alter the fact that I have been dreaming of going to the prom for my entire life, practically. And I really believe that I could achieve total self-actualization if you and I went to the prom together tomorrow night . . .'

Michael still looked like he couldn't quite believe any of it — that his band was actually being booked for a real gig; that that gig was the school prom; and that his girlfriend had just confessed that her way up the Jungian tree of self-actualization might be speeded along if he agreed to take her to said prom with him.

'Uh,' Michael said. 'Well, OK. I guess so. If you feel that strongly about it.'

I was so overcome with emotion that I reached out and grabbed Michael's head, just as I had grabbed Lana's. And just as I had done with Lana I dragged Michael's head towards me and planted a great big kiss on him . . . only not between his eyebrows, like with Lana, but right square on the lips.

Michael seemed very, very surprised by this — especially, you know, that I'd done it right in front of Mrs Weinstein. Which is probably why he turned red all the way to his hairline after I finished kissing him, and went, '*Mia*,' in a sort of strangled voice. But I didn't care if I'd embarrassed him. Because I was too happy. I went, 'See ya, Mrs Weinstein,' to Michael's stunned-looking English teacher and skipped out of there, feeling just like Molly when Andrew McCarthy came up to her at the prom and confessed his love to her, even though she was wearing that hideous dress.

And now I am sitting here — having told Lana that Skinner Box would definitely be performing at the prom — trembling with excitement over my own good fortune. I am going to the prom. I, Mia Thermopolis, am going to the prom. With my boyfriend and one true love, Michael Moscovitz. Michael and I are going to the prom.

MICHAEL AND I ARE GOING TO THE PROM!!!!!!!!!!!!!!!

TO THE PROM!!!!!!!!!!!!

PROM!

Homework:

Algebra: Who cares? Michael and I are going to the prom!!!!!

English: Prom!!!!

Biology: I'm going to the prom!!!!!!!!

Health and Safety: PROM!!!!!!!!!!!!!!!!!!!!!!!!!!!

Gifted and Talented: As if

French: *Nous Allons Au Promme!!!!!!*

World Civ.: WORLD PROM!!!!!!!!!!!!!!!!!!!!!!!!

PROM!

Friday, May 9, 7 p.m., the Loft

I really do not have time for all this bickering between my mom and Grandmère. Don't these women know I have more important things to worry about? I AM GOING TO THE PROM TOMORROW WITH MY BOYFRIEND. I am supposed to be getting plenty of rest and anointing my body with precious unguents right now, not refereeing fights between the post-menopausal and the hormonally-challenged.

WHY CAN'T YOU BOTH SHUT UP??????????? I want to scream at them.

But that, of course, wouldn't be very princesslike.

I am going to put on my headphones and try to drown out the noise with the mix Michael made for my birthday party. Perhaps the dulcet tones of The Flaming Lips will calm my fractious nerves.

Friday, May 9, 7:02 p.m.

Not even The Flaming Lips can drown out Grandmère's strident tones. Am switching to Kelly Osbourne.

Friday, May 9, 7:04 p.m.

Success! Finally, I can hear myself think.

Michael just emailed to let me know that he and the band would probably be up all night practising for their first big gig. But it is fully all right for the GUY to show up at the prom with dark circles under his eyes (look at that guy who ended up at the Time Zone dance with Melissa Joan Hart in *Drive Me Crazy*). It's just not OK for the GIRL to look less than petal smooth and daisy fresh.

The guys in the band aren't exactly stoked about the whole playing-at-the-prom thing. In fact, rumour has it Trevor even said, 'Oh, man, can't we just stick forks in our eyes, instead?'

But Michael says he told him a gig is a gig, and that beggars can't be choosers.

Michael signed off on his email with this:

See you tomorrow night. Love, M

Tomorrow night. Oh yes. Tomorrow night, my love, when I enter the prom on your arm, and see the jealous gazes of all my peers. Well, just Lana, because she's the only freshman besides me who is going. Except for Shameeka. Only she would never look at me jealously, because she is my friend.

Oh, and Tina. Because it turns out Tina is going to the prom too. Because of course Boris is in Michael's band, and since he is going to be there, he is allowed to bring one guest, and he chose Tina, because she, as he put it at lunch today, 'is my new muse, and sole reason for living.'

Oh, how thrilled Tina looked to hear those words uttered from the lips of her new love! I swear, she practically choked on her Fruitopia. She beamed across the table at Boris, and though I never thought I would write these words, I swear they are true:

Boris almost looked handsome as he basked beneath the hearthglow of her affection.

Seriously. Like, even his underbite didn't look that pronounced. And his chest kind of puffed out.

Either that, or he's been working out or something.

AHHHHH! The phone! Oh please God let it be my dad to say the strike is over and he's sending the limo down to pick Grandmère up . . .

Friday, May 9, 7:10 p.m.

It wasn't my dad. It was Michael, to ask if I agree with the line-up of songs Skinner Box plans on playing tomorrow. It includes many old prom standbys, such as The Moldy Peaches' 'Who's got the Crack' and Switchblade Kittens' 'All Cheerleaders Die', in addition to edgier stuff such as 'Mary Kay' by Jill Sobule and 'Call the Doctor' by Sleater-Kinney. This is not to mention Skinner Box's original songs, such as 'Rock-throwing Youths' and 'Princess of my Heart'.

I did feel compelled to suggest Michael substitute 'Rock Throwing Youths' with something a little less controversial, like 'When It's Over' by Sugar Ray or 'She Bangs' by Ricky Martin, but he said he would sooner show up in the middle of Times Square wearing nothing but a cowboy hat (oh, how I wish he would!). So I suggested some old school Spoon or White Stripes instead.

Then Michael went, 'What is all that shouting in the background?'

'Oh,' I said airily. 'That's just Grandmère and my mom arguing. Grandmère keeps insisting that my mom let her smoke in the Loft, but Mom says it's not good for me, or for the baby. Grandmère just accused my mother of being a fascist. She says when she had Hitler and Mussolini over

274

to the palace for tea at the height of World War Two, they both let her smoke, and if it was good for those guys, it should be good enough for my mom.'

'Uh, Mia,' Michael said. 'You do realize that your grandmother just turned sixty-five.'

'Yeah,' I said, remembering Grandmère's birthday with all too much clarity: she had insisted on me going back to Genovia with her to celebrate it, only I had had midterms (THANK GOD) and so was unable to. Don't think I didn't hear about THAT ad nauseam for weeks.

'Well, Mia,' Michael said. 'I know maths is not your strong point, but you do know that your grandmother could only have been about five years old during the height of World War Two. Right? I mean, she couldn't have had Hitler and Mussolini for tea at the Genovian Palace, because she wouldn't have even been living there yet, unless she married your grandfather when she was like, four.'

I was stunned into total and complete silence by that one. I mean, can you believe it? My own grandmother has been lying to me MY WHOLE LIFE. All Grandmère ever tells me about is how she saved the palace from being shelled by the Nazi hordes by having Hitler over for soup or something. All this time, I've thought about how brave she was, and what a diplomat, stopping the imminent military

275

incursion into Genovia with SOUP and her charming (well, back then, maybe) smile.

AND NOW I FIND OUT IT'S NOT EVEN TRUE?????????????????????????

Oh my God. She's good. *Really* good.

Although — and I never thought I would say this — it's sort of hard to be mad at her.

Because . . . well . . .

She did save the prom.

Friday, May 9. 7:30 p.m.

Tina just called. She is kvelling over getting to go to the prom. It is, she says, like a dream come true. I told her I couldn't agree more. She asked me how I thought we'd come to be so lucky.

I told her: Because we are both kind and pure of heart.

Friday. May 9. 8:00 p.m.

Oh my God. I never thought I would say this, but poor
Lilly.

Poor, poor Lilly.

She just found out that Boris is taking Tina to the prom.
She overheard Michael and I talking a little while ago. Lilly
is on the phone with me now, barely able to speak she is
trying so hard to hold back her tears.

'M-Mia,' she keeps choking. 'W-What have I d-done?'

Well, it is very clear what Lilly's done: ruined her life,
that's all.

But of course I can't tell her that.

So instead I went on about how a woman needs a man
like a fish needs a bicycle and about how Lilly will learn to
love again, blah blah blah. Basically all the same stuff Lilly
and I said to Tina back when she got dumped by Dave
Farouq El-Abar.

Except of course that Boris didn't dump Lilly: SHE
dumped him.

But I can't point this out to Lilly, as it would be like
kicking her when she was already down.

It is sort of hard dealing with Lilly's personal crisis when
a) I am so happy, and b) my mom and Grandmère are

still fighting in the background.

I just had to excuse myself for a moment and put the phone down. Then I went out into the living room and shrieked, 'Grandmère, for the love of God, would you please call Les Hautes Manger and ask them to hire Jangbu back so you can go return to your suite at the Plaza and leave us in PEACE?'

But Mr Gianini, who was sitting at the kitchen table, pretending to be reading the paper, went, 'I think it's going to take a little more than young Mr Pinasa getting his job back to end this strike, Mia.'

Which I must say is extremely disappointing to hear. Because I can barely find anything in my room, due to the fact that Grandmère's stuff is strewn everywhere. It is a little demoralizing to be looking around in my underwear drawer for a pair of Queen Amidala panties only to find the BLACK SILK AND LACE THONGS Grandmère wears. My *grandma* has sexier underwear than me. This is fully disturbing. I will probably be in therapy for years because of it too.

But no one seems to worry about the mental health of the children, do they? So when I came back into my room just now and picked up the phone Lilly was still going on about Boris. Really. It's like she doesn't even know I was gone.

'. . . but I just never appreciated what we had

together until it was gone,' she's saying.

'Uh-huh,' I go.

'And now I am going to grow old and die a spinster with maybe some cats or something. Not that there is anything wrong with that, because, of course, I don't need a man to be fulfilled as a human being, but, still, I always pictured myself with a live-in lover at the very least . . .'

'Uh-huh,' I go. I just now noticed to my extreme annoyance that Rommel has decided to use my backpack as his own personal bed. Also that Grandmère has very cavalierly draped her sleep mask over one of my Disney Princess snowglobes.

'And I know that I took him for granted and never even let him get to second base, but, seriously, he can't really think *Tina* is going to let him, can he? I mean, she is fully the type of girl who will demand a marriage proposal at the very least before she even lets him *look* under her shirt . . .'

Ooooh. This conversation suddenly got very interesting. 'Really? You and Boris never got to second base?'

'Well, it never really came up,' Lilly said, sounding very forlorn.

'What about you and Jangbu?'

Silence on the other end of the phone. *Guilty* silence, though. I could tell.

Still, it's good to know she and Boris never engaged in any full-frontal chestal activities. I mean, it will make Tina happy . . . as soon as I can get off the phone with Lilly and tell her, I mean.

I wonder if Michael and I will get to second base tomorrow night . . . after all, I'll be wearing my first strapless gown.

And it IS the prom . . .

Saturday, May 10, 7 a.m.

One would think that a PRINCESS would get to sleep in on the day of her first PROM.

BUT OH NO.

Instead of being wakened to the sound of birdsong, like princesses in books, I was wakened to the sound of Rommel shrieking as Fat Louie beat him senseless for getting into his bowl of Fancy Feast.

I am having a hard time summoning up any real sympathy for Rommel. After all, if it weren't for his behaviour on my birthday, he wouldn't be in this position right now. Although it is wrong to think Rommel could really have behaved any differently. He didn't exactly ASK Grandmère to bring him along to my birthday dinner. And it is clear to me now, having lived with him for several days, that Rommel, more than anyone I know, suffers from Asperger's syndrome.

Oh God. I can hear the Gorgon stirring even now . . .

Maybe if I go grab my prom dress and run out of the door now I can hightail it uptown to Tina's and prepare for my Big Night in the relative privacy of her place . . .

Oh my God. That's it. That's *exactly* what I'll do! Why

didn't I think of it before? I hate to leave my mom and Mr G alone with Grandmère all day again, but, really, what choice do I have? THIS IS THE PROM!!!!!!!!!!!!!!!

If ever there was a time for emergency action, this is it.

Saturday, May 10, 2 p.m.

Well, I did it. I escaped from Casa Horrifico.

Tina and I are safely ensconced in her room, having our pores unclogged by heat-action mud masks. We just had our nails done at Miz Nail down the street (well, I basically just had my cuticles done, since I don't really have any nails) and, in a little while, Mrs Hakim Baba's hairdresser is coming over to do our coiffures.

This is *so* how you are supposed to spend your Prom Day: beautifying yourself instead of listening to your mother and your grandmother bicker over who drank the last of the PediaLyte (Grandmère, it turns out, likes it with a splash of vodka).

Of course, I feel badly that my mother doesn't get to share in this very important day in my formative development as a woman. However, she has more important things to worry about. Such as gestating. And doing her breathing exercises, to keep herself from killing Grandmère.

Reports from the strike negotiations are not promising. Last time we turned on New York One, the Mayor was urging all New Yorkers to stock up on staples such as bread and milk, since we were no longer going to be able to turn to our local Chinese restaurants or pizzerias for sustenance.

Really, I don't know what Mr G and Mom and Grandmère are going to eat without delivery from Number One Noodle Son. They'd better hope they can pick up some prepared food at Jefferson Market . . .

Not that any of that is my concern. Not today. Because today, the only thing I am going to worry about is looking beautiful for the prom.

Because today, I am just like any other girl on her prom day. Today, I am a

PROM PRINCESS!!!!!!!!!

Saturday, May 10, 8 p.m., in the limo on the way to the prom

Oh my God, I am so excited I can barely contain myself. Tina and I look FABULOUS, even if I do say so myself. When the boys see us — we are meeting them at the prom, as they had to go early to set up — they are going to PLOTZ.

Of course, it does suck a little that Tina and I, instead of just having adorable little beaded clutches at our sides, have to bring along a couple of bodyguards. Seriously. They never mention this in the *Seventeen Magazine* prom issue. You know: How to Accessorize Your Bodyguard.

You should have heard Lars and Wahim grousing about having to get into tuxes. But then I reminded them that Mademoiselle Klein was going to be there, and that to my certain knowledge she was going to be wearing a dress with a slit up the side. That seemed to spark their interest, and they didn't even complain when Tina and I pinned on their matching boutonnières. They look so cute together . . . kind of like Siegfried and Roy. Minus the tigers, and fake tans and all.

I didn't mention that Mr Wheeton was going to be there too . . . and that, in fact, he'd be escorting Mademoiselle

Klein. Somehow, I didn't think that information would be very well received.

Oh my God, I am so nervous, I am actually SWEATING. I am telling you, fifteen is turning out to be the best age EVER. I mean, already I have got to play my first game of Seven Minutes in Heaven AND I'm going to my first ever prom . . . I truly am the luckiest girl in the world. Oh my gosh. WE'RE HERE!!!!!!!!!!!

May 10, 9 p.m., the Empire State Building Observation Deck

I never thought I would say this, but Grandmère rules.

Seriously. I am SO glad she brought Rommel to my birthday dinner, and that he escaped, and that Jangbu Pinasa tripped over him, and that Les Hautes Manger fired him, and that Lilly adopted his cause and created a citywide hotel, restaurant and porters' unions strike.

Because if she hadn't the prom might never have been cancelled, and Lana and the rest of the Prom Committee would have gone ahead and had it at Maxim's instead of being forced to have it on the observation deck of the Empire State Building — something arranged entirely by Grandmère, who is like *this* with the owner — and Michael would have continued to refuse to go to the prom at all, and so instead of standing under the stars in my totally rocking Jennifer Lopez-engagement-ring pink prom dress, listening to MY BOYFRIEND'S BAND, I'd be stuck at home, instant messaging my friends.

So as I stare out at the twinkling lights of Manhattan, all I can say is:

Thank you, Grandmère. Thank you for being such a complete freak. Because without you my dream of entering the prom on the arm of my one true love would never have come true.

And, OK, it kind of sucks that we can't dance because the only time there's any music is when Skinner Box is playing.

But the band took a break a little while ago, and Michael came over with a glass of punch for me (pink lemonade with Sprite in it . . . Josh tried to spike it, but Wahim totally caught him and threatened him with his nunchakus) and we went over to the telescopes and stood with our arms round each other, gazing out at the Hudson River, snaking silverly along in the moonlight, and . . .

Well, I'm not sure, but I think we got to second base.

I'm not sure because I don't know if it counts if a guy feels you up THROUGH your bra.

I will have to consult with Tina on this, but I think the hand actually has to get UNDER the bra for it to count.

But there was no way Michael was getting under MY bra, given as how I am wearing one of those strapless ones that are so tight it feels like you are wearing an Ace bandage around your boobs.

But he tried. I'm pretty sure, anyway.

There really is no doubting it now. I am a woman. A woman in every sense of the word.

Well, almost. Probably I should go into the ladies' room

289

and take this stupid bra off so if he goes for it again I might actually be able to feel something . . .

Oh my God, somebody's mobile is ringing. That is so rude. And in the middle of 'Princess of my Heart' too. You would think people would show some respect for the band and turn off their—

Oh my God. That's MY mobile!!!!!!!!!!!!!!!!!!!!!!!

Sunday, May 11, 1 a.m., St Vincent's Maternity Ward

Oh . . . my . . . God.

I can't believe it. I really can't. Tonight, not only did I become a woman (maybe) but I also became a big sister.

That's right. At 12:01 a.m., Eastern Standard Time, I became the proud big sister of Rocky Thermopolis-Gianini.

He is six weeks early, so he only weighed four pounds, fifteen ounces. But Rocky, like his namesake — I guess Mom was too weak to argue for Sartre any more. I'm glad. Sartre would have been a lousy name. The kid would have got beaten up all the time for sure with a name like Sartre — is a fighter, and will have to spend some time in an 'isolet' to 'gain and grow'. Both mother and Y-chromosomed oppressor, however, are expected to be fine . . .

Though I don't think the same can be said for the grandmother. Grandmère is slumped beside me in an exhausted heap. In fact, she appears to be half asleep, and is snoring slightly. Thank God there is no one around to hear it. Well, no one except for Mr G, Lars, Hans, my dad, our next-door neighbour Ronnie, our downstairs neighbour Verl, Michael, Lilly and me, I mean.

But I guess Grandmère has a right to be tired. According to my mother's extremely grudging report, if it hadn't been for Grandmère, little Rocky might have been born right there in the Loft . . . and with no helpful midwife in attendance, either. And seeing as how he came out so fast, and is so early, and needed a hit of oxygen before his lungs really started going, that could have been disastrous!

But with me away at the prom, and Mr Gianini having left the Loft to go 'buy some Lottery tickets down at the deli' (translation: he'd needed to get out of there for a few minutes, not being able to stand the constant bickering any more), only Grandmère was around when Mom's waters suddenly broke (thank God in her bathroom and not on the futon couch. Or else where would I sleep tonight????).

'Not now,' Grandmère apparently heard my mother wailing from the toilet. 'Oh God, not now! It's too soon!'

Grandmère, thinking Mom was talking about the strike, and that she didn't want it to end so soon because it meant she'd be deprived of the delightful company of the Dowager Princess of Genovia, of course went bustling into my mom's room to ask which newscast she was watching . . .

Only to find that my mother wasn't talking about something she'd seen on TV at all. Grandmère said she didn't even think about what she did next. She just ran out of the Loft, screaming, 'A cab! A cab! Somebody get me a cab!'

She didn't even hear my mother's mournful cries of, 'My midwife! No! Call my midwife!'

Fortunately our next-door neighbour Ronnie was home — a rarity for her on a Saturday night, as Ronnie is quite the femme fatale. But she was just recovering from a bout of the flu and had decided to stay in for the night. She opened her door and stuck her head out and went, 'Can I help you, miss?'

To which my grandmother apparently replied, 'Helen's in labour and I need a cab! And that's Your Royal Highness to you, mister!'

While Ronnie ran downstairs to flag down a cab, Grandmère ducked back into the apartment, grabbed my mom, and went, 'Come on, Helen, we're going.'

To which my mother supposedly replied, 'But I can't be having the baby now! It's too soon! Make it stop, Clarisse. Make it stop.'

'I can command the Royal Genovian Air Force,' Grandmère supposedly replied. 'As well as the Royal Genovian Navy. But the one thing in the world I have no control over, Helen, is your womb. Now come on.'

All this activity was enough to wake up our downstairs neighbour Verl, of course. He came running out of his apartment thinking that the mother ship was finally landing . . . only to find a mother of quite a different kind waddling down the stairs in front of him.

'I'll run to the deli and get Frank,' Verl said, when he learned what was going on.

So by the time Grandmère got my mom all the way down three flights of stairs, Ronnie had secured a cab, and Mr G and Verl were racing up the street towards them . . .

They all piled into the cab (even though there is a city ordinance that there are only five people, including the driver, allowed in a cab at one time – something the cabbie apparently pointed out, but to which Grandmère replied, 'Do you know who I am, young man? I am the Dowager Princess of Genovia and the woman responsible for the current strike, and if you don't do exactly as I say I'll get YOU fired, too!') and sped off to St Vincent's, which is where Lars and Michael and I found them (in the maternity waiting area – minus my mom and Mr G, of course, who were in the delivery room) half an hour after they called me, waiting tensely to hear if my mother and the baby were all right.

My dad and Hans joined us a little while later (I called him) and Lilly showed up a little after that (Tina had apparently called her from the prom, feeling bad for her, I guess, sitting around at home) and the nine of us (ten if you count the cabbie, who stuck around demanding somebody pay for the damage Ronnie's stilettos did to his floor mats, until my dad threw a hundred dollar bill at him and the guy grabbed it and took off) sat there watching the clock — me in my pink prom dress, and Lars and Michael in tuxes. We were definitely the best-dressed people at St Vincent's.

If I had any fingernails before, I certainly don't now. It was a VERY tense two hours before the doctor finally came out and said, with a happy look on her face, 'It's a boy!'

A boy! A brother! I will admit that I was, for the teeniest second, a little disappointed. I had been hoping for a sister so hard! A sister I could share things with — like how tonight at the prom, I had maybe got to second base with my boyfriend. A sister I could buy those cheesy plaques for — you know, the ones that say, 'God made us sisters, but life made us friends.' A sister whose Barbies I could still play with, and nobody could accuse me of being a baby, because, you know, they'd be HER Barbies, and I'd be playing with HER.

But then I thought of all the things I could do with a baby brother . . . you know, make him wait on line for *Star Wars* tickets, something no girl would ever be stupid enough to do (we'd use MoviePhone instead). Throw rocks at the mean swans on the palace lawn back in Genovia. Steal his *Spider-Man* comic books. Mould him into a perfect boyfriend for some lucky girl of the future, like in the Liz Phair song 'Double Dutch'.

And suddenly the idea of having a brother didn't seem so horrible.

And then Mr G came stumbling out of the delivery room, tears streaming down either side of his goatee, gibbering like those rhesus monkeys on the Discovery Channel about his 'son', and I knew . . . just knew . . . that it was right and good that my mom had had a boy . . . a boy named Rocky — after a man who, if you think about it, was really very respectful and loving of women ('Adrian!') . . . that my mom and I had somehow been divinely chosen for this. That together, Mom and I would raise the most kickass, non-sexist, non-chauvinistic, Barbie-AND-Spider-Man loving, polite, funny, athletic (but not a dumb jock), sensitive (but not whiny), second-base-getting-to, non-toilet-seat-leaver-upper that there had ever been.

In short, we would raise Rocky to be . . .

Michael.

Only I hereby swear, on all I hold sacred — Fat Louie; Buffy; and the good people of Genovia, in that order — that I will make sure that when Rocky is old enough to attend his Senior Prom he will NOT think it is lame to do so.

Sunday. May 11. 3 p.m.

Well, that's it. The strike is officially over.

Grandmère has packed up her things and gone back to the Plaza.

She offered to stay until Rocky comes home from the hospital, to 'help' my mom and Mr G with him until they get on some sort of schedule. Mr G couldn't seem to say, 'Um, thanks so much for the offer, Clarisse, but no,' fast enough.

I have to say, I'm glad. Grandmère would only get in the way of my moulding Rocky into the perfect boy. Like you can so tell she'll always be saying stuff to him like, 'Who's my big boy? Who's my gwate big widdle man?'

Seriously. You wouldn't think it of Grandmère, but when we finally got to see Rocky in his little incubator last night, that's exactly the kind of stuff she was saying. It was revolting.

I kind of know now why my dad has so many issues with forming lasting relationships with women.

Anyway, the restaurateurs finally caved in to the demands of the busboys. They will now all be receiving health benefits and sick leave and vacation pay. Well, all except for Jangbu, of course. He collected the money from his life story and flew back to Tibet. I guess city life didn't really work out all that well for him. Besides, in Tibet, all that money will provide him and his family with financial stability for life — not to mention a palatial mansion. Here in New York, it would have barely bought him a walk-up studio in a bad neighbourhood.

Lilly seems to be getting over her disappointment of not having gone to prom. Tina gave her a full report — about how after Michael unceremoniously abandoned the rest of the band in order to escort me to the hospital, Boris took over lead guitar, even though he'd never played the guitar before in his life.

But of course, being a musical genius, there is no instrument Boris can't pick up almost instantaneously . . . except for maybe like the accordion, or something. Tina says after we left things got a little out of hand, with Josh and some of his friends leaning over the side of the observation deck and seeing if they could hit stuff below with their own spit. Mr Wheeton caught them though, and gave them all in-school suspension. Lana supposedly started crying and told Josh he'd ruined the most special night of her life, and that this was how she was going to be forced to remember him when he went off to college next year . . . hawking loogies off the Empire State Building.

Sweet.

As for me, well, I don't have to worry: when Michael goes off to college next year

a) it will be just uptown, so I'll still see him all the time, anyway. Or at least, a lot of the time, and

b) the memory I'll have of him is not hawking loogies off the Empire State Building, but of turning to my dad in the maternity waiting room and saying (after I'd asked Dad, for the millionth time, if, now that I had a baby brother, I could stay in New York for the whole summer and get to know him, and Dad, for the millionth time, replying that I had signed a contract and had to stick to it), 'Actually, sir, legally, minors can't enter into contracts and so, according to New York State law, you cannot hold Mia to any document she might have signed, as she was under sixteen at the time, making it invalid.'

WHOA!!!!!!!!!!!!!!!!!! RIGHTEOUS!!!!!!!!!!!!!!!!!!!!!

You should have seen my dad's face! I thought he was going to have a coronary then and there. Good thing we were already at the hospital, just in case he keeled over. George Clooney could have rushed right over with the crash cart.

But he didn't keel over. Instead, Dad just looked Michael very hard in the face. I am happy to report that

Michael just looked right back at him. Then Dad said, all grimly, 'Well . . . we'll see.'

But you could tell he knew he'd been beat. Oh my God, it is so GREAT going out with a genius. It really is.

Even if he hasn't, you know, mastered the art of strapless bra removal.

Yet.

So I've finally got my room back . . . and it looks like I'll be staying in the city for at least the majority of the summer . . . and I have a baby brother . . . and I wrote my first actual story for the school paper, AND had a poem published . . . and I *think* my boyfriend and I might have got to second base . . .

And I got to go the prom.

TO THE PROM!!!!!!!!!!!!

Oh my God. I'm self-actualized.

Again.

About the Author

Meg Cabot (her last name rhymes with habit, as in 'her books-can-habit-forming') is the author of the phenomenally successful The Princess Diaries series — which has been published in more than thirty-eight countries and was made into two hit films — as well as several other series and bestselling novels for children, teenagers and adults. Her books have sold millions of copies around the world.

Meg has lived in various parts of the US and France, but now lives in Key West, Florida, with her husband and various cats.

www.megcabot.com

THE PRINCESS DIARIES

ROYAL REBEL

SCHOOL.

WITHOUT MICHAEL.

SERIOUSLY, WHAT IS EVEN THE POINT?

THE SIXTH BOOK IN THE HILARIOUS, BESTSELLING
THE PRINCESS DIARIES
SERIES

THE PRINCESS DIARIES

DIARIES

PARTY PRINCESS

SO – PARTIES. YOU JUST GO, MINGLE AND DANCE, RIGHT? BUT WHAT ARE YOU SUPPOSED TO DO ABOUT YOUR BODYGUARD?

GOD. THIS PARTYING THING IS GOING TO BE HARDER THAN I THOUGHT.

THE SEVENTH BOOK IN THE HILARIOUS, BESTSELLING
THE PRINCESS DIARIES
SERIES

THE PRINCESS DIARIES

ROYAL SCANDAL

OH MY GOD, WHO AM I FOOLING?
I CANNOT DO THIS!!! I'M A *PRINCESS*,
FOR CRYING OUT LOUD.

AND AS A PRINCESS, I WILL ALWAYS
VALUE QUALITIES SUCH AS HONESTY
AND SELF-RESPECT AND NOT-DOING-IT-
WITH-PEOPLE-YOU-DON'T-EVEN-LOVE.

THE EIGHTH BOOK IN THE HILARIOUS, BESTSELLING
THE PRINCESS DIARIES
SERIES

THE PRINCESS DIARIES

BAD HEIR DAY

PANIC WAS RISING IN MY THROAT. IT WAS SORT OF THE WAY I FELT EVERY TIME I THOUGHT ABOUT MICHAEL, ONLY WITHOUT THE SWEATY PALMS.

'I CAN'T DO THIS. I CAN'T GIVE A SPEECH IN FRONT OF TWO THOUSAND SUCCESSFUL WOMEN. YOU DON'T UNDERSTAND – I'M GOING THROUGH A ROMANTIC CRISIS.'

THE NINTH BOOK IN THE HILARIOUS, BESTSELLING

THE PRINCESS DIARIES

SERIES